Enid Blyton

STORIES OF
WONDERS
AND
WISHES

Look out for all of these enchanting story collections
by Enid Blyton

Animal Stories
Cherry Tree Farm
Christmas Stories
Christmas Tales
Christmas Treats
Christmas Wishes
Fireworks in Fairyland
Magical Fairy Tales
Mr Galliano's Circus
Nature Stories
Pet Stories
Rainy Day Stories
Springtime Stories
Stories for Bedtime
Stories of Magic and Mischief
Stories of Mischief Makers
Stories of Rotten Rascals
Stories of Spells and Enchantments
Stories of Wizards and Witches
Stories of Wonders and Wishes
Summer Adventure Stories
Summer Holiday Stories
Summertime Stories
Tales of Tricks and Treats
The Wizard's Umbrella
Winter Stories

Enid Blyton

STORIES OF WONDERS AND WISHES

Illustrations by Mark Beech

HODDER

HODDER CHILDREN'S BOOKS

This collection first published in Great Britain in 2022
by Hodder & Stoughton

1 3 5 7 9 10 8 6 4 2

A CIP catalogue record for this book is available from the British Library.

ISBN 978 1 444 96542 1

Typeset by Avon DataSet Ltd, Alcester, Warwickshire

Printed and bound in Great Britain by Clays Ltd, Elcograf S.p.A.

The paper and board used in this book are made from
wood from responsible sources.

Hodder Children's Books
An imprint of Hachette Children's Group
Part of Hodder & Stoughton
Carmelite House
50 Victoria Embankment
London EC4Y 0DZ

An Hachette UK Company
www.hachette.co.uk
www.hachettechildrens.co.uk

Contents

The Wish That Came True   1

The Magic Bicycle   9

The Astonishing Curtains   19

The Grand Birthday Cake   27

The Flopperty Bird   39

The Wonderful Garden   47

The House in the Fog   53

The Magic Brush   69

The Very Strange Pool   77

The Silly Little Conker   85

The Boy Whose Toys Came Alive!   91

A Pennyworth of Kindness   111

The Astonishing Ladder   121

The Impossible Wish   135

The House Made of Cards   141

The Salt, Salt Sea 151

The Goblin in the Train 157

The Box of Magic 165

The Unlucky Little Boy 177

The Little Silver Hat 183

The Toys' New Palace 191

Blackberry Magic 203

Foolish Caryll 215

The Treasure Hunt 221

The Little Old Toymaker 227

Sally Suck-A-Thumb 237

A Wonderful Thing 247

His Little Sister 253

In the King's Shoes 261

The Ship in the Bottle 273

The Two Good Fairies 291

The Wonderful Conjurer 301

Acknowledgements 307

The Wish That Came True

The Wish That Came True

PIPPY AND Flip were flying their big kite. It pulled at its string as hard as it could.

'It's a fine kite,' said Pippy. 'It flies well.'

'It will bump into that cloud if it doesn't look out,' said Flip. 'There – it has, and it's taken a little corner out of it too.'

'Let me hold it for a bit,' said Pippy. So he held it and enjoyed feeling the tug and pull of the eager kite far away up in the sky.

'Pippy! Flip!' called their mother. 'It's dinnertime. Come along quickly. Haul down your kite and put it away.'

'Oh no, Ma!' called Pippy. 'It's flying so well. Can't we tie it up and leave it to fly?'

'No,' said his mother. 'Pull it down. You know we're going over to old Dame See-Saw after dinner, and we'll have to run to catch the bus, I expect. Pull your kite down at once.'

'Don't let's,' whispered Pippy. 'Let's tie it to something and it can fly all the time we're having dinner. It will love that.'

'What can we tie it to?' asked Flip. 'Ooh, I know – let's tie it to Ma's old garden chair. That will hold it well while we are having our dinner.'

So they tied it to their mother's old garden chair and then went in to their dinner. But while they were having their dinner, the wind grew very much stronger. It was almost a gale. *Whooooooooooo-hoooo-hooo*, it went, and the kite tugged hard at its string. The old garden chair gave a sudden little hop. The kite had pulled so hard that it made it move. The kite tugged at its string again and the chair gave another little hop.

Then the wind blew so hard that the kite tugged wildly – and will you believe it, up into the air went the old garden chair, swinging at the end of the long, long string!

The kite flew higher in the sky and further away. The chair hopped over the wall and flew up into the air too, and it even flew over the roof of a cottage. My word, it was having the time of its life!

It flew and it flew, and then – dear me, the knot in the string began to come loose! Soon the chair would fall. It might break itself into pieces. It began to be afraid.

The wind dropped a little, and the kite flew lower. The chair dropped lower too, and almost touched a wall it was swinging over. Suddenly the knot came undone, and the string parted from the back of the chair.

But it hadn't really very far to fall. It fell into a little garden, behind a bush, and there it stood, feeling shaky, wondering where it was.

Now old Dame See-Saw had been hanging out her washing on that lovely windy day. She had washed all the morning, and she was very, very tired. It was nice out in the garden, and she thought she would like a little rest out there.

If only I had a garden chair to rest in and to ease my tired old legs, wouldn't that be lovely! she thought, pegging up the last stocking. *How I wish I had a comfortable old garden chair for myself!*

Plop! Something fell down that very moment behind the nearby bush. Dame See-Saw was startled. She went to see what it was.

'Bless us all – it's an old garden chair, dropped right out of the blue, as I wished my wish!' she said in astonishment. 'Well, there now – it's just what I want to sit in and rest my old legs. I'll have a little snooze.'

So down she sat and shut her eyes. The chair was so comfortable and fitted her exactly. 'It couldn't be better,' she said sleepily. 'Oh, how lovely to have a wish come true! I really must tell Pippy and Flip and their mother when they come to see me.'

Well – they're on their way in the bus, of course. And what *do* you suppose Pippy's mother will think when she sees old Dame See-Saw fast asleep in the old garden chair that really belongs to *her*? And what will Pippy and Flip say?

Well, if ever a wish came true, Dame See-Saw's did that afternoon. And if I know anything about her, she's going to keep that chair!

As for the kite, it's still flying. Look out for it. It's black and blue, with a smiling face and a tail made of yellow and red. I'll let you know if I see it!

The Magic Bicycle

The Magic Bicycle

PETER HAD a lovely new bicycle for his birthday. It was painted bright red with a yellow seat, and on the handlebars was a bright silver bell. It was a fine bell, and had a very loud ring. You should have seen everybody jump when Peter cycled up and rang it just behind them.

Peter went out on his bicycle every day after school, just before tea. It was great fun cycling up and down the lane, ring-ringing all the way.

But one afternoon a strange thing happened to Peter. He was cycling along whistling happily to himself, watching rabbits scamper along the grassy verge.

When he came to the little hill that ran down to the sweetshop at the bottom, he took both his feet off the pedals and had a lovely ride – but, do you know, when he reached the bottom of the hill the bicycle wouldn't stop.

No, it went on, all by itself without Peter doing anything to help it. He was so surprised.

What a funny thing! he thought. *What's happened to my bicycle, why is it going by itself? Ooh! It's going faster! My goodness, I hope we don't run into anyone.*

On and on went the little red bicycle, with Peter holding on tightly. It went faster and faster, and Peter had to hold on tightly to his cap, in case it blew away.

The bicycle raced through the village and made everyone jump quickly out of the way. It nearly knocked over Mr Plod, the policeman. Poor Peter couldn't possibly say he was sorry because the bicycle didn't stop.

On and on it went, up hills and down hills, along the country lanes, past fields and farmyards. At last the little red bicycle ran into a village Peter had never seen before. It was a strange place. The houses all looked like doll's houses, and there was a farm exactly like Peter's toy farm in the bedroom at home, with funny wooden-looking trees standing in rows, and wooden-looking cows grazing in the fields.

And what do you think were in the street? Why, toys, all standing about and talking to one another, or shopping busily.

'This must be Toy Town,' said Peter to himself in astonishment. 'Perhaps my bicycle came from here and felt homesick suddenly, and raced back home.'

In the middle of the street was a wooden policeman, holding up his hand to stop the traffic. The bicycle tried to get past – but the policeman grabbed the handlebars and stopped it. Off fell Peter, landing with a bump.

'Why didn't you stop?' cried the policeman crossly. 'Didn't you see my hand put out?'

'Yes, but my bicycle wouldn't stop,' said Peter.

'It won't do what I tell it to!'

'I don't believe a word of it,' said the policeman, getting out his notebook. 'Show me your bicycle licence, please.'

'But I haven't got one,' said Peter in surprise. 'You don't need to have a bicycle licence where I come from – you only have licences for motorcars and television sets.'

'In Toy Town you have to have a licence for bicycles too,' said the policeman sharply. 'You must come to the police station with me, and pay a fine.'

'But I haven't any money,' said Peter, quite frightened.

'Never mind,' said the policeman. 'You can pay your fine in chocolate money instead.'

'I don't have any chocolate money either,' wailed Peter. But it made no difference. The policeman took him by the arm, and marched him down the street.

Suddenly there came a great noise of shouting not far off, and a big brown teddy bear rushed by, carrying a little bottle of brightly-coloured sweets.

'Stop thief, stop thief!' cried a little wooden shopkeeper dressed in a stripy apron. And all the toys standing around in the street began to chase the teddy bear, but he jumped into a toy motorcar and whizzed off at top speed.

Two more toy policemen rushed up. 'Who has another motorcar that we can use to chase him?' they cried. But nobody had. Then Peter had an idea.

'I'll go after him on my bicycle!' he said. 'Jump up behind me, policemen, and I'll scoot after that naughty teddy.'

In a second he was back on his bicycle, and behind him crowded the three wooden policemen, and another teddy bear who wanted to join in the fun.

Peter pedalled as fast as he could, and soon he could see the teddy bear up ahead of him in the toy motorcar.

The teddy looked behind him and saw that he was being chased. He went faster still, but Peter pedalled as hard as he could and soon he had nearly caught up.

Suddenly the clockwork motorcar the teddy was driving began to run down. It went slower and slower, until finally it stopped. The teddy got out to wind it up again – but before he had given it more than one wind, Peter had pedalled alongside.

The policemen jumped off and grabbed the naughty teddy. They made him give up the bottle of sweets and said he must clean the whole sweetshop from top to bottom to show that he was sorry.

'Well,' said the wooden policeman who had stopped Peter when he first arrived in the little village, 'that was a very good idea of yours, to let us chase that teddy on your bicycle.'

'That's quite all right,' said Peter. 'I was glad to help.'

'Thanks very much anyway,' said the policeman. 'I won't say any more about your not having a bicycle licence. You can go home now – but please be sure to have a licence if you come to Toy Town again.'

'Thank you,' said Peter, sitting down on the grassy roadside. He was very hot and tired after his long cycle ride. 'It's been a great adventure. But I do wish I didn't have to cycle all the way home again. This bicycle of mine won't seem to go by itself any more, and I shall have to pedal it up all of those hills.'

'Dear me, I didn't think about your being tired,' said the policeman, very much upset. 'Look here, get into this car with me – the one the teddy used. You can put your bicycle in the back. Can you drive a car?'

'No,' said Peter, 'not even a toy one, I'm afraid.'

'What a nuisance,' said the policeman. 'I can't drive either.' Then the clever policeman had a wonderful idea.

'Hey, Teddy Bear!' he cried to the miserable bear who was still being marched off down the road. 'You can drive this car, can't you? You can do something else useful to make up for all the trouble you've caused.'

'Oh! Yes,' said the bear, pleased to show how clever

he was. 'Jump in, everyone, and I'll drive Peter all the way home, if he will tell me where he lives.'

Off they all went, right through Toy Town and back to the village where Peter lived. How his friends stared when they saw him drive up with three wooden policemen and two teddy bears – but before they could ask them any questions the toys had driven off again, and Peter was left standing by his gate with his little red bicycle.

'What an adventure,' he said. And it certainly was, wasn't it?

The Astonishing Curtains

The Astonishing Curtains

MARY HAD a lovely doll's house. When Grandma gave it to her for her birthday it was quite new and empty. Grandpa gave her one pound to buy furniture for it, and Auntie Susan gave her fifty pence to buy curtains.

Mary went to the toy shop and spent the pound. She bought a little wooden table for the kitchen and two chairs to match. She bought a kitchen stove and dresser and some tiny saucepans and a kettle.

She bought little beds for the bedrooms, and wardrobes and chairs. She even bought a washstand for the biggest bedroom of all. The dining room had a round table, four chairs and a sideboard, and the drawing room had a fine carpet, a sofa, three pretty chairs and a tiny table.

Well, you wouldn't think she could get all those for a pound, would you? But she did, because the things only cost three or four pence each, and, as I daresay you know, there are one hundred pence in one pound, which is really rather a lot to spend all at once!

'Don't buy the stuff for the curtains today,' said Nurse. 'You'll have plenty to do arranging all the things you've bought. We will buy the curtains another time, and then I will help you to make them, and hang them up. You can keep Auntie Susan's fifty pence until you want to buy the curtains.'

Mary arranged all her new furniture in the doll's house, and it did look nice. It took her four days to get it all in and to lay the carpets and bits of oil cloth. Then she took out her fifty pence piece, and decided to buy the stuff for the curtains.

She spun it on the nursery floor – but, oh, dear me, when it stopped spinning, it rolled away and disappeared down a hole in one of the boards by the wall. Mary called Nurse, but they couldn't get it.

'No, it's gone,' said Nurse. 'It's a mouse hole, I expect, and unless we have some boards taken up, you won't get your money back again. I'm sure your daddy won't have the boards up, so you must make up your mind that it's gone for good.'

Tears came to Mary's eyes.

'What about the curtains for the doll's house?' she said. 'I've finished it all except for those – and Grandma and Auntie Susan are coming next week to see my house all finished.'

'Well, you shouldn't have been so careless as to lose your fifty pence,' said Nurse. 'I told you to put it safely in your moneybox.'

She went out of the room and Mary sat down on the floor and cried. It really was too disappointing for anything. She did so badly want pretty red curtains to hang at the windows of the doll's house.

That night, when the nursery was quiet, and Mary

had gone to bed, the toys in the cupboard came trooping out. And dear me, they were so cross with the little clockwork mouse!

'It's all your fault that Mary lost her fifty pence,' said the panda angrily.

'What do you mean?' asked the clockwork mouse in surprise.

'Well, your friend, the little brown mouse from the garden, made that hole to come into the nursery and visit you,' said the panda, pointing to the hole. 'And it was down his hole that Mary's money went. If you hadn't wanted that mouse to come and see you, he wouldn't have made that hole, and Mary wouldn't have lost her fifty pence!'

The clockwork mouse was dreadfully upset. He began to cry, and the toys tried to stop him, because they were afraid his tears might rust his spring.

'I w-w-wish I c-c-could get M-M-Mary some nice n-n-new curtains!' he sobbed. 'I'm so s-s-sorry about it.'

'If only we could get some stuff, I could make them

on that little toy sewing machine Mary had for Christmas,' said the biggest doll. 'It wouldn't take me long, because I know quite well how to use it.'

'Well, where can we get some stuff?' asked the clockwork mouse eagerly. 'I know Mary wanted red curtains – where can we get something that is red?'

'I know!' cried the teddy bear. 'What about the red creeper leaves that grow over the garden shed? If we got some of those, we could make lovely curtains from them for Mary.'

'But how can we get them?' asked the clockwork mouse.

'We'll ask your friend, the little brown garden mouse, to get them for us,' said the doll. So when the mouse popped up through the hole, they told him all about Mary and the lost fifty pence, and asked him to get the red leaves. First of all he tried to get the money out of the hole, but he couldn't. When he found it was no use, he ran off to get the red creeper leaves. He came back with two beautiful ones in his mouth and then ran off for more.

The sewing machine began to hum as the doll made the curtains. As soon as a pair were made the teddy bear and the panda took them to a window and put them up. You can't think how lovely they looked!

Just as the cock crowed at dawn, the last pair were finished and the toys went happily back to the toy cupboard.

And in the morning, when Mary came running into the nursery, oh, what a surprise she had! She stood and stared at the doll's house with its bright red curtains as if she really couldn't believe her eyes! And when she saw that they were made of red creeper leaves, she looked round at her smiling toys in wonder.

'You must have made them for me!' she said. 'You darlings!' She hugged them all tightly, and they were as pleased as could be.

'Now the house is all ready for Grandma to see!' Mary cried. 'And the curtains are the prettiest part of all!'

The Grand Birthday Cake

The Grand Birthday
Cake

HELEN LIVED in a little house that stood next to a very big one. In the big house lived three children, and they had fine games together. Helen used to watch them from her bedroom window and wish that she could play too.

Helen had no brothers or sisters. She lived alone with her grandmother, and because they were very poor she had hardly any friends. Her granny did not like her to ask other children to tea because it meant buying cakes and she said she couldn't afford it. So Helen played alone and it was very dull indeed.

She loved watching the three children next door.

They were so happy, so kind to one another, and they had so many toys! There was a seesaw in the garden, a swing and a little swimming pool – so you can guess they had plenty to do! When Helen saw the three children looking at her, she always looked the other way. She blushed because her dress was darned and mended, and her shoes so old. She felt sure that the three children would laugh at her if she gave them a chance. Their clothes were so lovely, and they always looked so pretty and clean.

One day Helen heard the children talking about a birthday party. It was for Kitty, the youngest little girl. She was going to be five, and was to have a very grand birthday indeed.

'You were ill on your birthday last year, Kitty,' said Mary, the eldest girl. 'So this year we are going to give you a perfectly marvellous party to make up for last year!'

'Ooh!' said Kitty in delight. 'How lovely!'

'You're going to have a great big birthday cake with

five fairies on it, each one holding a candle for you,' said Gillian, the other girl. 'And after tea there will be a conjuror doing tricks! And there is to be a bran-tub with a present for everyone in it – you too, Kitty!'

'Ooh!' said little Kitty again, her face red with delight.

Helen could hear everything that was said. How she wished she could go to a party like that! Fancy – a birthday cake with five fairies on it holding candles! And a conjuror! And a bran-tub with presents for everyone!

Saturday was the day of the party, when Kitty was five. Helen saw the postman go that morning with heaps of brown paper parcels and cards, and she guessed they were for lucky Kitty.

I wish I could see that birthday cake with fairies on, she thought longingly. *I expect they will be made of sugar and they will be lovely. I wonder if I could peep in at the window and see it.*

Kitty had one present she loved very much – and

that was a brown and white spaniel puppy! Her father gave it to her and she shrieked with delight.

'I shall put a ribbon round his neck because he is my birthday dog,' said Kitty. So she tied a big red ribbon round the dog's neck and then took him out into the garden to play. Helen saw them and thought the little dog was a dear.

That afternoon many children came to the house next door, all dressed up for the party. Helen could hear them playing games in the big room at the back.

I expect they will have tea in the dining room at the front of the house, she thought to herself. *It will be laid there. Oh, I wonder if the curtains are drawn! If they aren't I could just peep in at the window and see that birthday cake!*

Helen slipped on her coat and ran down to see. No, the curtains were not drawn! What luck! The little girl tiptoed her way into the front garden next door and went up to the big window. She peeped in – and oh, what a lovely tea table there was, just inside! You should have seen the cakes and buns, the biscuits and the jellies! And right in the very middle of the table was the birthday cake!

It was even lovelier than Helen had imagined. It was big, and was iced with pink and white sugar. On the top in the middle were five fairies, proper little dolls, not made of sugar, but dressed in silk, with silver wings. Each one carried a candle of a different colour!

Helen looked and looked – and then she saw something that made her open her eyes wide. The puppy had just run into the room. He stopped and smelt all the good things on the table. His brown nose twitched in excitement. What a lot of things to eat!

He jumped up on a chair and ate a plate of sandwiches – and then he saw that birthday cake. How he longed to lick it! Helen felt certain he was going to eat the cake, fairies and all, and she gave a scream. She rushed up the steps to the front door and hammered on it loudly. The children's mother opened it in surprise.

'Oh, please, Mrs White, your puppy is just going

to eat that lovely birthday cake!' panted Helen. 'I saw him through the window!'

Mrs White rushed into the dining room and the puppy jumped off the table at once. She looked at the birthday cake. One candle was broken – but the cake was all right! She saw the empty plate where the sandwiches had been and she scolded the puppy.

'Naughty little dog!' she said. 'You must learn not to steal! You might have spoilt the party! I don't know what Kitty would have said if you had spoilt her cake. She would have cried her eyes out!'

She quickly put another candle in the place of the broken one, and before she went to the kitchen to make some more sandwiches she turned to speak to Helen. But the little girl had slipped out, rather frightened to find herself in the big house, alone in a room with Mrs White.

'Dear me, bless the child, she's gone!' said Mrs White. 'Funny little shy thing! Gillian! Gillian! Come here a minute, will you!'

Gillian came running in, her eyes bright with excitement. It was a lovely party. Her mother told her what had happened and how Helen had run off before she could be thanked.

'Shall we send her in a piece of the birthday cake, Gillian?' said Mrs White. 'She always seems such a lonely little girl to me.'

'Oh, Mummy, she must be a dear!' said Gillian. 'Fancy coming in like that to save our birthday cake! Oh, Mummy, do let me go and bring her back to the party! We've always wanted to know her, she looks so sweet and kind, but she just looks away when we want to smile at her!'

'Very well,' said Mrs White, smiling at her kind-hearted little daughter. 'Fetch her in – but she may not want to come, Gillian, for I think her grandmother is very poor and I expect Helen has no party dress.'

'Well, she can wear my old one, then!' said Gillian, dancing about in glee. 'It will fit her nicely!'

Off she went to the little house next door and rang the bell. Helen opened the door, and stared in surprise at Gillian, all dressed up in silver and blue.

'Helen, thank you so much for saving our birthday cake!' cried Gillian. 'Please, we want you to come to Kitty's birthday party, oh do, do, do! We've wanted to know you for a long time, but you wouldn't look at us!'

'Oh – I can't come,' said Helen, blushing red. 'I've no party dress.'

'I've thought of that,' said Gillian, taking hold of Helen's hand. 'You can wear my old one, it's perfectly good except it's too small for me. Come on, I want you to come!'

'But – but – but,' said Helen, simply longing to go, but feeling dreadfully shy.

'What are you saying so many buts for?' cried her grandmother. 'Go, child, go! It will do you good!'

So Helen went. Gillian gave her her old party dress of pink and it fitted Helen beautifully. Gillian found a pink ribbon which Helen tied in her hair, and then she slipped a pair of dancing shoes, which also belonged to Gillian, on her feet. Then she was ready. Down she went to the party, and soon everyone knew that she was the little girl who had saved the birthday cake from being eaten.

What a fuss they made of her! It was such fun! They played games until teatime and then they all went in to tea. The candles on the cake were alight and how lovely the fine fairies looked, each holding one! Their silver wings glittered and their little faces shone in the candlelight. All the children cheered and Kitty went red with joy. It was the loveliest birthday cake she had ever had!

After tea there was the conjuror and he was very clever indeed. Then there was the bran-tub – and there was a present for Helen, though she hadn't expected one at all – and what do you think it was? Guess!

It was one of the fairies off the birthday cake! Helen couldn't believe her eyes. She looked at the beautiful little doll in delight – the nicest toy she had ever had!

'Oh, thank you, Mrs White!' she said. 'I do love it!'

'You deserve it!' said Mrs White, smiling. 'Now, mind you come and play in the garden with Gillian, Mary and Kitty whenever you can. They will love to have you, and you mustn't be lonely any more!'

So now Helen has three good friends and every day she plays in the garden next door. They have a lovely time, especially when Spot the dog joins them. Helen is very fond of him. 'You see,' she says, 'if it hadn't been for Spot I'd never have known you all, would I?'

The Flopperty Bird

The Flopperty Bird

THE FLOPPERTY bird belonged to Winky the gnome. It was a big bird, with lovely long tail feathers. Winky was very proud of it, and looked after it well. One day the flopperty bird said, 'You are good to me, Winky. You may pull one of my tail feathers out, and make a wish with it!'

Winky was excited. He pulled a feather out, and called his friend Longshanks the giant over to help him make a wish.

'What will you wish for?' asked the giant.

'Something you can share with me,' said Winky, 'because you gave me the flopperty bird when it was a chick.'

They decided to wish for something they were both very fond of. 'I wish for a big raspberry tart!' said Winky.

There was a thud behind them, and an enormous tart, steaming hot and smelling delicious, appeared. They set to work, and soon finished it.

'Thank you for sharing it, Winky,' said the giant. 'Now I must go home, or my wife will be cross.'

He was late for dinner, and his wife, who was a witch, was very cross indeed. 'Sit down and eat your dinner at once!' she snapped.

'Oh, dear, I don't want any,' said the giant. 'I'm not hungry!'

'What have you been eating?' asked his wife. The giant told her.

'What!' she cried. 'You wasted a wish on a raspberry tart!'

'A fine wish it was too!' said the giant. 'In fact, I'd like another one!'

'You might have had gold, or a palace or a kingdom!' stormed the witch.

The giant said nothing more, but the witch thought and thought.

'If the flopperty bird has any more wish feathers, it's no good silly Winky or big Longshanks having them,' she decided. 'I shall have them!'

So that night she took a big pair of scissors, crept into Winky's cottage, and with one snip cut off all the other tail feathers of the poor flopperty bird. He woke up and began to squawk, while the witch rushed away into the darkness.

When she got home she went down to the cellar. She had eight feathers, which she flung one by one into the air, each time saying, 'I wish for a bag of gold!' Immediately eight large sacks of gold appeared. Crowing and chuckling, the witch went to bed.

Winky and Longshanks were terribly upset about the flopperty bird's tail feathers, but as hard as they searched, they couldn't find out who had taken them.

Then one day Longshanks began to wonder why his wife kept disappearing so often.

He followed her quietly the next time she went down to the cellar. And there he stared in amazement at the sacks of gold, for he guessed it was his wife who had taken the flopperty bird's feathers. He ran to tell Winky and the bird.

'Take me to her!' said the bird. They surprised the witch, who was still in the cellar.

'I don't care!' she said, laughing. 'I've got my sacks of gold!'

'You haven't!' cried the flopperty bird and he laughed loudly.

'See!' said the witch, and shook a sack open. Out poured a stream of yellow grain! The magic had gone from the gold!

'Aha!' said the bird. 'I think, as you have such nice corn, Mistress Witch, I'll stay a few weeks with you and feed on it, for then my tail will grow again!'

So he did, and each time the witch fed him, the

flopperty bird gave her a good peck, just to teach her that greediness never did anyone any good!

The Wonderful Garden

The Wonderful Garden

THERE WAS once a school in the middle of a big town. It had a large concrete yard for a playground, with not a blade of grass and certainly not a flower. The park was so far away that many of the smaller children had never seen a flower growing in the earth.

The teacher, Miss Thomas, was sad about it. 'Do you know,' she said to her mother, 'some of my little ones have never seen a flower growing, or a butterfly or even a bee! Isn't it dreadful?'

'You must put that right,' said her mother. 'Get the children to help you and try to make a garden for them!'

So Miss Thomas spoke to the children, and they made a plan. Some of them had dirty little back yards. Two of them had tiny gardens where a bush or two grew. One of them knew the park keeper, because he was a friend of her father's. Between them they decided to do a very hard thing. They would make a garden in their school yard!

The children who had dirty little back yards scraped up earth from them and carried it to school in bags and pails. The two that had tiny gardens borrowed a barrow and wheeled earth to school in it. The one who knew the park keeper asked her father to beg for any soil he could spare when he was digging up the beds in the park. Little by little a mound grew in the sunniest corner of the school yard. It grew and it grew. It was added to each day by some child or other. Miss Thomas nearly wore her arms out carrying earth from her home to the school. But at last there was enough in the mound to plant some seeds in!

What excitement there was! The children bought

marigold seeds, nasturtium seeds, candytuft and poppies. They planted them after a rain shower. In a week all the seeds were showing tiny green heads. They grew higher – they made themselves leaves. They put up buds! The children loved them and watered them when they were dry.

Then the flowers opened, and the little corner was bright with orange marigolds, golden nasturtiums, red and pink and white poppies and pretty candytuft. Everybody in the school looked at the tiny garden at least twenty times a day. The people who lived in the dull, dirty houses around came and peeped through the railings at it.

And do you know, the bees found it! They came from the faraway park, and hummed happily all day long in the children's flowers. The butterflies found it, and fluttered about the school playground for the first time in years. And one day a robin saw it, and he sat on the school wall and sang a dreamy little song about flowers and sunshine!

'It's a tiny bit of countryside right in the very middle of the town,' said everyone. 'It was well worth the aching arms and heavy loads! Who would have thought that we could bring growing flowers, humming bees, colourful butterflies and singing birds into our dirty old yard!'

I'd like to see that garden, wouldn't you? It's wonderful what people can do when they all work together!

The House in the Fog

The House in the Fog

THERE WAS once a boy who didn't believe in fairies, or pixies, or giants, or dragons, or magic or anything like that at all.

'But at least you know there were dragons,' said Mary. 'St George killed one. It's even in our history books at school, where it tells us why we have St George's cross on our flag.'

'Believe what you like,' said William, 'I just don't think there ever were such things.'

Now one day William had to go to a Cub meeting. He was a very good Cub indeed, and meant to be an even better Scout later on. He had his tea at home then looked at the clock. 'I must go, Mother,' he said. 'I've got to be at the meeting at six.'

His mother peered out of the window. It was a dark evening – and, dear me, how foggy it seemed too! 'I wonder if you ought to go, William,' she said. 'It's getting foggy.'

'Oh, Mother – what does that matter?' said William, putting on his Cub jersey. 'I know my way blindfolded! I can't *possibly* miss my way home.'

Well, William was certainly a very sensible boy, so his mother let him go. He got to the meeting in good time – William was always punctual – and he had a very nice evening. Then it was time to go home.

The Cubmaster looked out of the door. 'My word,' he said, 'the fog is very thick. I hope you will find your way home all right.'

'Well, we all go the same way, except William,' said John. 'So we can keep together. What about William, though?'

'Pooh!' said William. 'Do you suppose I'd lose my

way in a fog! A Cub knows his way about even if he can't see a thing!'

And off he went out into the fog alone. Didn't he know his way perfectly well? Hadn't he walked the same road dozens of times? What did it matter if the fog was thick? He could *easily* find his way home.

But after he turned two corners he suddenly stopped. His torch hardly showed a beam at all in the thick fog. Was he on the right road? He must be! He couldn't possibly have taken the wrong turning.

He flashed his torch on the name of the road, printed on a wall nearby. Ah, yes – he was all right – it was Ash Tree Avenue. Thank goodness! He hadn't gone the wrong way after all.

'I've only to go down to the end of the road, turn sharply to the left, cross over, and then keep straight on until I get to my own house,' said William to himself. So off he went again, his steps tap-tapping in the fog which now swirled thickly about him.

He went on and on. Wherever was the end of Ash

Tree Avenue? Surely it wasn't as long as this! On and on and on. William stopped, puzzled. He ought to have come to the end of it by now, and have turned left.

He turned and went back. *I'll start at the top again, where the name of the road is*, he thought. His steps tap-tapped again as he went. On and on and on he walked.

He didn't come to the beginning of the road, where he had seen the name. Where was it? He had kept on the very same pavement and he hadn't crossed over at all. It *must* still be Ash Tree Avenue. But why didn't it end? He stopped again. He turned and went *down* the road this time. Surely he would come to the turning! On he went, but there really was no turning! What had happened?

'I'm not in a dream, I know that,' said William. 'I've just come from the Cub meeting, and I'm walking home in rather thick fog. And I'm on the right way. I'm not lost. I just can't seem to find the end of this road.'

It was no use. He couldn't find it. No matter if he went up or down, there seemed no end and no beginning.

'This is absolutely silly,' said William at last. 'There's no sense in it. I shall go into one of those houses and ask my way.'

He flashed the torch on the gate of the nearest house. He saw the name there: MUNTI HOUSE. He went up the little path and came to the front door. It had a peculiar knocker in the shape of a man's head. The head had pointed ears and a wide grin. William knocked on the door with it.

The door opened, and a dim light shone out from the hall. 'Please,' began William, 'could you tell me—'

Then he stopped. Nobody was there. There was just the open door and the dark hall and nothing else. How peculiar! William peered inside.

A curious whistling noise came from the hall, like the wind makes in the chimney. 'Well,' said

William, 'if someone is whistling, someone is at home. I'll go in.'

So in he went and the door shut softly behind him. He walked up the hall and came to a room without a door. Someone was whistling there. The whistling stopped. 'Come in, come in,' said a high little voice. 'What do you want, William?'

William jumped. How did anyone in that house know his name? He looked round the room in surprise. A plump little man with pointed ears and remarkably green eyes was sitting in a rocking chair by an enormous fire. Rockity-rock, he went, rockity-rock. He looked at William and grinned.

'Why,' said William, 'you are exactly like the knocker on your door!'

'I know,' said the little man. 'Why shouldn't I be? Your name's William, isn't it? I'm Mr Munti, of Munti House.'

'How do you know my name's William?' asked William.

'Well, I just took one look at you and I knew your name must be William,' said Mr Munti, rocking furiously. 'That's easy.'

It didn't seem easy to William. He stared at Mr Munti, who stared back. 'I came to ask if you could . . .' began William, but he was interrupted by a large black and white cat with eyes as green as Mr Munti's.

'MEEEE-ow,' said the cat, walking into the room and patting Mr Munti on the knee. 'MEEEE-ow!'

'Hungry, are you?' said Mr Munti. 'Pour, jug, pour!'

There was a pint milk jug on the table and, on the floor below, a large saucer. The jug solemnly tipped itself and poured milk into the saucer below.

'Good, jug, good,' said Mr Munti, rocking away hard. 'You didn't spill a drop that time. You're getting better.'

William stared in surprise. What a peculiar jug! He looked at Mr Munti. 'I say,' he said, 'are you a conjuror?'

'No,' said Mr Munti. 'Are you?'

'No,' said William. 'I'm a little boy.'

'Don't believe in them,' said Mr Munti, and he gave a sudden high chuckle like a blackbird. 'I never did believe in little boys.'

William was astonished. 'But you *must* believe in them,' he said. 'I've just been to a Cub meeting. I'm a Cub, and I...'

'There you are!' said Mr Munti, grinning. 'You're a Cub. You're not a little boy. What sort of Cub are you? I believe you're a fox cub. You've got such a nice bushy tail.'

William felt something swishing behind him and looked around. To his enormous astonishment he saw that a fine bushy tail hung down behind him. He turned round to see it properly – and the tail turned with him. He felt it – good gracious, it seemed to be growing on him, right through his trousers!

'MEEEE-ow,' said the cat again and patted the little man on the knee.

'What! Still hungry?' said Mr Munti. 'I never knew such a cat! There's a kipper in the cupboard for you.'

The cat went to the cupboard door, stood on his hind legs and opened it. He sniffed inside the cupboard, put in his paw and pulled out a kipper. It landed on the floor.

'Shut the door, Greeny, shut it,' ordered Mr Munti. The cat blinked at him with deep green eyes and carefully shut the cupboard door. Then he began to eat his kipper.

William stared, open-mouthed, forgetting his tail for the moment. What a clever cat!

'Well?' said Mr Munti, rocking away hard. 'Did you say you were a fox cub? Or perhaps you are a bear cub? I see you have nice hairy paws.'

William looked at his hands in horror. Whatever was the matter with him? He had big hairy paws now, instead of hands. He hid them in his pockets at once, full of dismay. What *was* happening? What was this little man with the bright green eyes?

'No – on the whole, I think you must be a lion cub,' said Mr Munti, peering at him. 'I never in my life have seen such wonderful whiskers. Magnificent. Aren't they, Greeny? Even better than yours.'

'MEEEE-ow,' said Greeny, and began washing himself very thoroughly.

William felt his face in alarm. Goodness gracious, there were long strong whiskers growing from his cheeks – how very peculiar he must look! His paw brushed against his face, a furry, soft paddy-paw, just like a bear's.

'Please, sir,' said William, beginning to feel scared, 'I want to go home. I'm not a lion cub, or a bear cub or a fox cub – I'm a little boy Cub, a sort of Scout.'

'I told you, I don't believe in little boys,' said Mr Munti. 'So I don't believe in your home either. I don't believe you want to go there because there isn't one, and I don't believe in *you*. Do you believe in me?'

'Well – what are you?' asked William desperately.

'My mother was a pixie and my father was a magical

brownie,' said Mr Munti, rocking away.

'Then I don't believe in you,' said poor William. 'I don't believe in fairies, or pixies, or magical brownies, or dragons, or giants or . . .'

'And I don't believe in little boys, so we're quits,' said Mr Munti with a wide grin.

'Ding-dong,' said the clock loudly, and danced all the way down to the end of the mantelpiece and back again.

'Will you stop that?' said Mr Munti fiercely to the clock. 'How often must I tell you that well-behaved clocks don't caper about like that?'

William began to feel bewildered. His tail waved about behind him. He could feel it quite well. His hairy paws were deep in his pockets. He could feel the whiskers on his cheeks. *What* was happening? He didn't believe in any of it, but it was happening all right – and happening to him.

'I'm going out of this peculiar house,' said William suddenly and he turned to go.

'You might say goodbye,' said Mr Munti, rocking tremendously hard and almost tipping over.

'Goodbye, Mr Munti,' said William.

'MEEEE-ow,' said the cat, and came with him to the front door. The cat stood up and opened the door politely. William went out into the darkness and the fog. The door shut. He shone his torch on the knocker head, and then on the name of the house on the front gate – MUNTI HOUSE. Who was Mr Munti really? Was he, *could* he be a conjurer? Conjurers did do peculiar things. But that cat too – and the jug – and the clock!

'I shall certainly come back tomorrow and see Mr Munti again, in the daylight,' said William to himself. He went down the road, hoping that he would find the end of it this time. And, to his great delight, he did. The fog began to clear a little, and he could see his way.

'Turn to the left – then over the crossing – and straight home!' said William in delight. 'Oh, dear –

what in the world will Mother say when I arrive home with a tail and furry paws and whiskers?'

She didn't say anything – because when William thankfully walked in his tail had gone, his hands were his own again and there were no whiskers left. And what was more, his mother wouldn't believe a word of his tale!

'Fancy you making up such a silly story!' she said. 'You're very late, William – and you needn't tell me a lot of fairy tales like that. Just tell the truth.'

Now, the next day, as you can imagine, William went off to Ash Tree Avenue to look for Munti House, and the strange knocker on the door and Mr Munti himself. And will you believe it, though he looked at every single house in the avenue at least three times, not one was called Munti House, and not one had a knocker in the shape of a grinning head.

Poor William was terribly puzzled. He told his story to several people, but nobody believed him at all. 'How *can* you make up such a story when you've always said you don't believe in things like that?' said Mary.

He told it to me. That's how I know about it. 'I've no tail left, of course,' said William, 'but see, there are a few little hairs still on my hands, and there's a place on my left cheek that feels a bit like a whisker growing. Do, do tell me what you think about it, please?'

Well, I don't know what to think! What do you think about it all?

The Magic Brush

The Magic Brush

ONCE UPON a time Dame Lazybones went to do a little spring cleaning at Wizard Twinkle's castle. She was just like her name, and never did a thing unless she had to.

Now, when she got to the castle Wizard Twinkle was just going out. 'Good morning, Dame,' he said. 'Please scrub all the floors today – and do them well!'

He slammed the great door, and Dame Lazybones sighed and groaned. How dreadful to have to do so much work all at once! Then she spied something that made her chuckle with delight. The wizard had left out his magic book of spells. The dame ran to it and looked up 'Scrubbing brush'. She soon found what she wanted.

'To make a brush scrub by magic,' she read, 'take an ordinary brush, lay it down on its back, trip round it three times, cry "Romany-ree" as you go, and then kick the brush in the air, saying "Scrub away, brush!"'

In great delight the woman took the scrubbing brush, laid it down on its back, and tripped round it three times, crying loudly 'Romany-ree!' Then up into the air she kicked the brush, shouting 'Scrub away, brush!'

The brush fell to the ground and then, to Dame Lazybones's great delight, it began to scrub the floor all by itself. You should have seen it! There was a large pail of soapy water just nearby, and the brush kept going to this and dipping itself in, and then scrubbing the floor with a fine, *shishoo-shishoo-shishoo* noise.

'Ah,' said Dame Lazybones, sitting herself down in the wizard's own armchair with a pleased smile. 'This is the best way to work – sitting down and watching something else!'

Well, it wasn't long before the dame was fast asleep, and she snored gently while the scrubbing brush went on working busily. It finished the floor of that room and went to the next. Then it went upstairs and did the bedroom floors. They were all of stone, and very dirty indeed, so the brush really did work hard.

At last all the floors were finished. The brush sat up on its end and looked round for something else to scrub. Ah yes! It would scrub the walls.

So it began. But it didn't like the pictures that hung here and there so it sent those down with a crash to the floor. That woke up Dame Lazybones, and she looked at the brush in horror.

'Stop! Stop!' she shouted. 'Whatever are you doing?'

But the brush didn't stop. It began scrubbing the top of the stove and sent five saucepans, three kettles and a frying pan flying off with great clangs and bangs. Dame Lazybones rushed to the magic book and looked up the spell again – but to her great dismay there was nothing there about how to stop a magic brush from working. She didn't know what in the world to do. She rushed at the brush just as it was going into the larder, and tried to snatch it.

Crack! It gave her such a rap on the knuckles. She tried to get hold of it again, and once more it tapped her smartly on the hand. Then it popped into the kitchen cupboard and began to scrub the shelves, sending everything flying out into the kitchen.

'Oof!' said Dame Lazybones as a milk pudding landed on her shoulder. 'Ow!' she cried as a jelly slipped down her neck. Crash! Smash! Down went dishes of jam tarts, tins of cakes, joints of meat on the floor – and dear me, a large bottle of milk crashed down near the surprised kitchen cat, who at once began to lick it up with joy.

'Stop! Stop!' cried Dame Lazybones in horror to the excited brush. But nothing would make it stop! It went next to the windows and began to scrub those, and down came all the curtains on the floor.

And just at that moment the door opened and in came Wizard Twinkle! Oh my, how Dame Lazybones shivered and shook.

'Oh, stop the brush, stop it!' she cried. But the wizard shook his head. 'It has one more job to do!' he said – and as he spoke, the brush flew over to poor Dame Lazybones and began to scrub her too! Oh, what a state she was in! How she ran, how she fought that brush – but it wasn't a bit of good, it gave her a good drubbing, rubbing and scrubbing!

Then the wizard clapped his hands and said, 'Romany-ree, come to me!' The brush hopped over to him, stood by his foot and did nothing more.

'See what your laziness has done!' said the wizard, looking all round with a frown at the dreadful mess everywhere. 'You will now clean up this place from top to bottom, Dame Lazybones – and never let me hear of your being *lazy* again!'

'Oh, no sir, no sir!' wept Dame Lazybones as she

hurried to pick up all the things lying on the floor. 'Oh, I'll never be lazy again! Oh, that dreadful brush! Oh, deary, deary me!'

And you'll be glad to know that the old dame never *was* lazy again; she couldn't forget that magic brush!

The Very Strange Pool

The Very Strange Pool

NOW ONCE upon a time Shiny-One the gnome had to take a heavy mirror to Dame Pretty. It was a very large looking glass indeed, bigger than Shiny-One himself, so it made him puff and pant, as you can imagine.

When he got to the middle of Cuckoo Wood he felt that he really *must* have a rest. So he laid the mirror flat on the ground, with the bracken and grass peeping into it, and went to lean against a tree a little way off. And he fell fast asleep.

Now along that way came little Peep and Pry, the two pixies who lived at the edge of the wood. They were always peeping and prying into things that were no business of theirs – so you can guess they were most astonished to see a big flat shining thing in the middle of the wood!

'Look at that!' said Peep. 'A new pool!'

'A lovely, shiny pool!' said Pry. They both ran to it – and indeed, the mirror did look exactly like a shining pool of clear water, for it reflected the grass, the bracken, the trees and the sky exactly as a sheet of water does.

'I wonder how a pool suddenly came here,' said Peep. 'It's really rather extraordinary. There was never one here before.'

'It hasn't been raining,' said Pry. 'I just can't understand it. Do you suppose it is a magic pool, Peep?'

'Yes – perhaps it is,' said Peep.

'Peep – shall we take a little drink from it, in case it's a wishing pool?' whispered Pry.

'Well – do you think we'd better?' said Peep. 'Suppose it belongs to somebody?'

'They'll never know,' said naughty Pry. 'Come

on – let's scoop a little water up in our hands and drink it. We'll wish at the same time.'

Peep put his hand down to the mirror – but, of course, all he felt was something hard, and not soft water! He stared in astonishment.

'The pool's frozen!' he said. 'Look – there's no water – only ice.'

'Well, that *shows* it's magic!' said Pry at once. 'That just shows it is! How could water freeze on a warm autumn day like this? It's impossible.'

'I think you're right,' said Peep in excitement. 'Yes, I really think you are. A pool that is frozen hard on a warm day *must* be magic! Whoever it belongs to must have frozen it so that nobody could take a drink and wish.'

'Ah – but we can manage to trick the owner!' said Pry in a whisper. 'We can break the ice, Peep – and drink the water below! Can't we?'

'Of course!' said Peep. 'Come on – let's break it, and drink quickly, before anyone comes.'

So they took stones and banged the pool hard – crack! The mirror broke into little pieces – and to the pixies' great astonishment there was no water underneath!

'Stranger and stranger!' said Peep. 'I wish there was somebody we could tell this to.'

Then they saw Shiny-One the gnome, not very far off, just waking up. They ran to him.

'I say, there's a magic pool over there!'

'We knew it was magic because it was frozen hard.'

'So we cracked the ice to get a drink of the water underneath – but there wasn't any! Did you ever know such magic?'

'What nonsense are you talking?' said Shiny-One crossly. He knew Peep and Pry well and didn't like the way they poked their noses into things that had nothing to do with them. 'A magic pool – frozen on a day like this! Rubbish!'

Peep and Pry took him to the pool – and Shiny-One stared down in horror at his poor broken mirror.

'My mirror!' he said. 'The one I was selling to Dame Pretty. Look what you've done, with your silly interfering ways – smashed that beautiful big mirror! You bad pixies! How much money have you got in your pockets? You'll have to pay for that mirror.'

Peep and Pry tried to run away – but Shiny-One caught hold of them both. He turned them upside down and shook them well. All their money rolled out of their pockets.

'Thank you,' said Shiny-One, and he turned the pixies the right way up. 'Thank you! Just enough to pay for a new mirror, I think. Now run off before I think of chasing you all the way home.'

Peep and Pry ran off, crying. Shiny-One dug a hole with a stick and buried all the bits of broken mirror, so that nobody's feet would get cut.

As for Peep and Pry, they couldn't buy sweets for four weeks, because all their money had gone – so maybe they won't go poking their noses about quite so much another time!

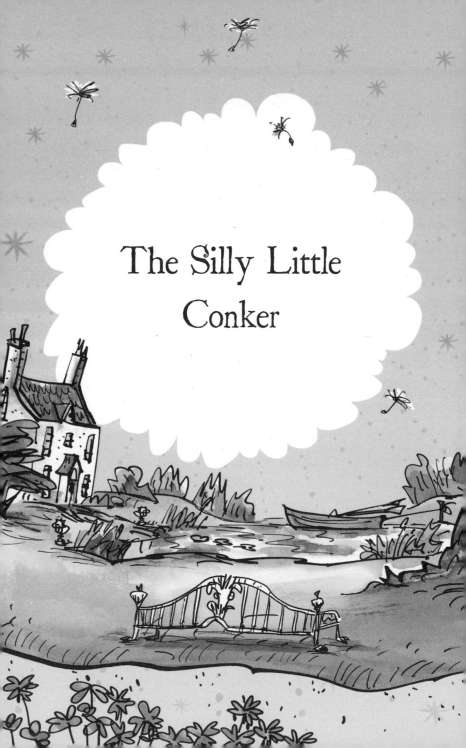

The Silly Little Conker

The Silly Little Conker

THERE WAS once a big chestnut tree that was always full of conkers in the autumn.

Two boys came one day with a barrow, and they picked up a big load of conkers, all in their prickly cases. When they got home they put all the conkers on the table and began to take them out of their cases. They were looking for some specially good ones to play 'conkers' with at school.

'I say! What a fine lot of big conkers these are!' said Will. 'The best we've ever had!'

'Yes!' said Peter. 'I'm sure we shall beat all the others when we play conkers with these!'

They sorted them out. There was only one small conker among them. Peter flipped it off the table.

'We don't want *that* silly little conker!' he said. The conker rolled away into a corner and lay there, miserable and forgotten.

The next day the baby found it, as she played on the floor, and she was very pleased with it. 'Look, Mummy, a conker!' she said.

Her mother made a hole in it and put it on a string for her to play with. But when Peter and Will came home from school, very proud because their big conkers had beaten everyone else's, they took the little conker away from the baby. 'It's such a silly little conker,' said Will. 'Look, you shall have a nice big one, Sheila!'

The little conker was quite in despair. It had been happy with the baby, and was pleased even when she sucked it. Now it was no use at all. Will took it up and swung it round and round on the string. 'I'll throw it out of the window!' he said.

So out of the window it went, string and all. It fell with a thud on to the damp piece of ground, just where there was a gap in the garden hedge. How it envied all the other conkers in the playroom, having a fine time with Will and Peter!

It lay there forgotten. The frost bit it. The rain wetted it. Birds hopped over it, and once a rat came and smelt it. Then, in February, the conker began to feel rather strange. It had been rained on for a week and it was very wet. It swelled up to twice its size till the hole through its middle was quite closed up. Then something grew out of it down into the ground. It was a root! After that something grew up into the air – a strong little shoot!

When the springtime came the little conker had fallen away almost to nothing, for the root and the shoot had fed on it, and, lo and behold, there was a sturdy little chestnut tree, just putting out a fan of green leaves at the top. The two boys found it one day and cried out in glee!

'Mother! Look! Here's that silly little conker we threw away! It's grown into a lovely little tree which will just fill the gap in the hedge! Isn't it fine! Look, the string is still through it! All the big conkers are dried up and useless now, but this one will be a tree and grow conkers of its own!'

The tiny tree waved in the wind, full of content. What did it matter being silly once, when it could be wise all the rest of its life!

The Boy Whose Toys Came Alive!

The Boy Whose Toys Came Alive!

THERE WAS once a boy called Sammy, who longed for his toys to come alive.

'I'm sure you come alive at night and have a lovely time!' Sammy said to them. 'Well, why can't you come alive and really play with me in the daytime? Oh, I do wish you would!'

But they didn't – until something peculiar happened. It was like this. Sammy was walking along the lane to his home when a tiny rabbit flung itself out of the hedge and crouched down at Sammy's feet. After the rabbit came a fierce little weasel.

Sammy was frightened – but he picked up the

little rabbit and held it safely in his arms. 'You go away!' he said to the weasel. Just as he spoke, a small magical brownie came running from the hedge, and ran up to Sammy.

'Oh, you've saved my pet rabbit for me!' he cried. 'Thank you a thousand times, Sammy! Snowball escaped this morning from her hutch, and I knew the weasel would be after her. Come here, you silly little Snowball!'

Snowball leapt from Sammy's arms into the brownie's. The little man petted and scolded her. Then he spoke to Sammy.

'I do feel so grateful to you for saving my pet rabbit. Is there anything I can do for you in return?'

Well, you can just guess what Sammy thought of at once! His toys!

'Yes, there is something you can do for me,' he said. 'Make all my toys come alive! Can you do that?'

'Yes, I can,' said the brownie. 'But just tell me this first – are you a good boy or a naughty one?'

'Does that matter?' asked Sammy, going red. He

was a naughty boy, not very kind to others, often disobedient, and so noisy that his mother, who was not very well, was always having headaches.

'Well, it does matter a bit,' said the brownie. 'You see, your toys will behave like *you* when they come alive. It wouldn't do to have a nursery full of bad toys, you know. You'd get very tired of them. Also, you must promise not to tell anyone they are alive.'

'Of course I promise!' said Sammy. Then he told a story. 'I'm a good boy!' he said. 'So do make my toys come alive!'

'Very well,' said the brownie. He felt in his pocket and brought out a little tin. 'Rub this yellow ointment on to your toys,' he said. 'It will make them all come alive.'

Sammy was so excited that he forgot to say thank you. He tore off home with the tin and rushed up to his playroom. Which toy should he make come alive first?

'I'll make my clown come alive!' he said. So he rubbed a little of the ointment on to the clown's face.

It acted like magic! The clown yawned, got up and ran round the nursery at once! Sammy could hardly believe his eyes. This was simply fine!

'Come here, clown,' he said. 'I want to have a look at you. Come and speak to me.'

'Don't want to,' said the clown, 'I want to play with the bricks.'

'Come here at once when I tell you!' said Sammy angrily. Do you know, that clown turned and made a very rude face at Sammy!

Sammy was so angry that he ran after him. And that naughty little clown turned round and pinched Sammy in the leg! Then he ran off and got behind the toy cupboard so that Sammy couldn't reach him.

'All right, you just wait!' said Sammy. He went to where he had left his tin of ointment and picked it up. He rubbed some on to his soldiers, his teddy bear, his sailor doll, his train, his horse-and-cart, his red ball and his bricks!

Well, you should have seen the playroom after

that! The soldiers at once began to march in splendid rows, and the soldier band began to beat the drum and blow the trumpets! It sounded beautiful.

The teddy bear chased the sailor doll, and the train shot round the playroom so fast that it bumped into the box of bricks. But the bricks were alive and sprang out of their box at once. They hopped about, and threw themselves here and there joyfully. One brick threw itself at the teddy bear and hit him on the nose. The bear was angry and ran after all the bricks, which hopped about the floor like mad things, making a tremendous noise!

'Stop that noise!' said Sammy, who was afraid his mother would come in. But do you suppose those bricks stopped? Not a bit of it! They danced about all the more, and two of them threw themselves at Sammy and hit him on the head!

Then the train got excited and ran over Sammy's foot. Its key caught his ankle and hurt him. Sammy held his foot and hopped about in pain.

'He thinks he's one of the bricks hopping about!' cried the sailor doll rudely. 'Just look at him!'

Sammy bent down and shoved the sailor doll – and the doll gave a howl of rage, ran to the workbasket on the window seat, took out a needle and pricked Sammy in the leg with it.

'Ow! Ow-ow!' yelled Sammy, hopping round again, first on one foot and then on the other. How his toys laughed!

Then the horse-and-cart began to gallop round the playroom – and you should have seen the horse kick up its little wooden legs! And how it neighed too! Sammy would have loved to listen if only it hadn't made quite such a noise!

'You do make a noise,' he grumbled. 'Oh, goodness me – now that ball's begun bouncing itself! I say, don't bounce so high, ball! Do you hear me? Don't bounce so high!'

The ball squeaked for joy and went on bouncing just as high as it wanted to. It bounced so high that it struck a vase of flowers – and over went the flowers, and down went the vase on to the floor, crash!

Well, all this noise was really too much for Sammy's mother. She was resting downstairs, and she called up to Sammy, 'Sammy! Come here! What was that you broke just now?'

Sammy went down to his mother, looking cross and worried. 'I didn't break anything,' he said. 'The ball bounced up and knocked down the vase of flowers.'

'Oh, Sammy, that was very naughty of you,' said Mother.

'Mother! I didn't do it!' cried Sammy. 'It was the ball, I tell you.'

'Don't talk like that,' said his mother. 'And don't be silly. Balls don't bounce themselves.'

But that was just what Sammy's ball *was* doing, wasn't it! Sammy went back upstairs, very cross and upset.

'Here he comes! Here he comes!' he heard his toys say as he came in at the door. They were all waiting for him.

The ball bounced up into his face and hit his nose. The bricks, which had built themselves up into a high tower, made themselves fall all over him. The clown pinched at his left leg and the teddy bear pinched at his right one. The sailor doll pulled his laces undone. The train tried to run up his leg. The horse galloped his cart over Sammy's left foot and back again in a most annoying way, and all the soldiers ran at him and tried to poke through his socks with their swords.

'What are you all doing, you bad toys?' cried Sammy.

The toys danced round in glee, shouting and squealing.

'You were never kind to us!' yelled the bear. 'We're having fun now you've made us come alive!'

And then the clown did a silly thing. He saw the tin of yellow ointment where Sammy had left it on the chair – and he ran to get it.

'I'm going to make the chairs and tables come alive!' he yelled. 'Watch me, toys!'

And then, to Sammy's horror, that naughty clown

ran to the table and rubbed some yellow ointment on to its legs. Then he rubbed some on to the chairs and then smeared some on the cushions, the fender, the stool, the lamp and everything else he could think of!

'Stop, stop!' shouted Sammy. But it was too late – the whole of the playroom was alive!

Goodness, you never heard such a noise as that furniture made! The table at once began to dance round and round, first on one leg and then on the others. The chairs played 'Catch' with one another, and banged all round the room trying to grab each other with their legs.

The lamp tried to get out of their way and bumped into the stool, which was very angry and kicked at the lamp.

The fender began to laugh and stood itself up on end to see how tall it was. All the cushions rolled off the chairs, and tried to flop on top of the toys.

Sammy stood by the wall, looking quite frightened.

It was like a bad dream. The armchair raced by and bumped into him. Sammy fell down at once, and all the other chairs raced over him. The fender laughed so much that it fell down with a crash.

'This is awful,' said Sammy, trying to get up out of the way of the stool, which seemed to think it would like to stand on Sammy's middle. The fender stood itself up again to see better. A large blue cushion flung itself on top of the surprised teddy bear, and he sat down hard, with a growl. The fender laughed so much that it fell down again.

'*Silly* fender!' said Sammy, feeling very angry with it. 'Stop laughing!'

But the fender couldn't. Then the train began to laugh too – the engine, the carriages and the rails – and they made such a noise skipping about and squealing, that Sammy felt quite certain his mother would be angry enough with him to send him to bed for the rest of the day.

'Listen, toys! Listen, everyone,' said Sammy, trying

to make them stop. 'I shall get into such trouble if you behave like this! I never knew such a noisy, disobedient nursery! Wherever in the world do you get these bad manners from?'

'You!' screamed the toys. 'We've learnt it all from watching *you*! That's why we're noisy! That's why we're rude and disobedient! That's why we're unkind! You taught us!'

The clock on the mantelpiece suddenly struck twenty-one without stopping and walked up and down like a policeman. The fender began to laugh again, and down it fell with a crash.

This time it fell on the clown, who was so hurt that he yelled the place down.

'Stop screaming like an express train!' cried Sammy angrily. 'I know you'll bring my mother up here! Oh, how I wish I'd never made you come alive, you tiresome things!'

'Well, we *are* alive, so you'll have to put up with it!' said the teddy bear rudely.

'If you talk to me like that I'll punish you!' shouted Sammy. He ran to punish the bear, and the fender stood itself up again to see the fun. But before Sammy could punish the teddy, the clown neatly tripped him up and down he went with a bang. The fender almost choked with laughing and fell down with a worse crash than usual.

Sammy kicked the fender. He kicked the stool. He kicked the engine and the red ball. He kicked everything he could reach, for he was in a terrible temper.

And then the toys and everything else decided that they would do a little kicking too. After all, if you are a table with four legs, you can do a lot of kicking! So they all rushed after Sammy, and the table got four fine kicks in all at once. Sammy gave a yell and rushed out of the room.

'After him, after him!' shouted the table, and tried to get through the door. But it got mixed up with the fender, who was hopping along to see the fun, and it was a good half minute before they got outside the door. Then the fender laughed so much that it fell down again, and the table jumped over it and left it there on the landing.

Now Sammy had rushed to his room and locked the door, but the nursery things didn't know this. They thought he had run downstairs. So down they all went, helter-skelter, after him. Well, really, you never heard such a noise!

The table clattered down on all four legs, and the chairs jumped two stairs at a time. The coal scuttle rolled itself down and made a great noise. The stool hopped down, and the cushions rolled over and over. The fender stopped laughing, and slid itself down, bump-bump-bump, from stair to stair. It was enjoying itself thoroughly.

The clown and the rest of the toys rushed down after the furniture. They all had to pass the open door of the room where Sammy's mother was trying to rest.

She saw the table gallop past, and she was most

astonished. She thought she must be dreaming.

Then the chairs hopped by, and Sammy's mother sat up and stared. Then the lamp rolled by and the stool trotted along behind.

Am I really seeing tables and chairs running along? Why are they running along? Where are they going? Oh, dear, it really makes me feel ill! thought Sammy's mother.

The fender came along and stared in at the room. When it saw Sammy's mother looking so frightened it began to laugh, and down it fell with such a crash that Sammy's mother nearly leapt off the sofa. The fender picked itself up and hopped on after the others. Then the toys raced along too, and the engine clattered by with its carriages. The ball bounced along and the bricks hopped merrily. It was really an alarming sight.

Sammy was trembling in his bedroom. He heard everything racing by, and he wondered what his mother would say if they all went into her room – and then he heard them out in the garden! He went to his window and looked out.

'Where's he gone?' cried the clown.

'He must be down the lane!' growled the teddy bear.

'After him!' shouted the lamp – and out of the garden gate they all went.

Well, they made such a noise that the magical brownie who lived in the lane peeped out to see what it was all about. And when he saw the live toys and furniture, he guessed at once what had happened.

'They must belong to Sammy – and he used his yellow ointment on them!' he cried. 'Oh my, he must have been a bad boy to have such noisy, naughty toys! I shall have to do something about this!'

He ran into the lane and spoke to the toys and the furniture.

'What's all this? What's all this? Please walk by me, one by one, slowly and without noise.'

Everything was afraid when they heard the brownie's stern, rather magical voice. So one by one they went quietly by him – and quickly he dabbed each toy and each piece of furniture with a blue ointment.

When every one of them had gone by, the brownie called to them sternly. 'In two minutes you will no longer be alive. You had better go quietly back to Sammy's playroom unless you want to be left out in the lane.'

What a shock all the toys and the furniture got! They were so afraid of being left out of doors that they all turned round and rushed up the lane, through the gate and into the house. And Sammy's mother saw them all again, rushing the *other* way this time!

'I'm dreaming again!' she said. 'Oh, dear, I must be ill or something. And here's that dreadful fender staring at me again, and laughing!'

Sure enough the fender began to laugh, and it laughed so much that when it fell down with a crash at the bottom of the stairs, it couldn't get up again. And the two minutes were up before it could climb the stairs, so there it stayed, quite still.

But all the other things got safely into Sammy's playroom and just had time to arrange themselves in their places before the magic worked. They gave a sigh, and stayed as still as could be. There wasn't a growl from the teddy nor was there a creak from a chair!

When everything was quite quiet, Sammy unlocked his door and peeped out. He tiptoed to his playroom. He saw that everything was quite still. He wondered if he could possibly have dreamt it all – but no, there was the little tin of yellow ointment still on the chair.

'Horrid stuff!' cried Sammy. He picked up the tin, put on the lid, and then threw it as far as ever he could out of the window!

If my toys behave like me, then I must be a very bad boy! thought Sammy to himself. *I'll try and be a bit better in future. Oh, goodness – here's Mother! I'm sure she will be cross with me.*

Sammy was right – she was! She had made up her mind that Sammy must have thrown all the furniture and toys downstairs and then thrown them up again!

'What a bad, naughty boy you are, Sammy!' she said. 'What do you mean by throwing everything downstairs? And do you know you've left the fender at the bottom of the stairs and I nearly fell over it! You will go straight to bed and stay there.'

'Yes, Mother,' said poor Sammy, trying to be good and obedient for once. He went to his room, but on the way he peeped down the stairs and saw the fender at the bottom.

'You can stay there!' said Sammy. 'Laughing like that! I suppose you thought it was all very funny!'

The fender tried to laugh but it couldn't. Sammy went to bed, very sad and sorry.

And so far nobody has found that tin of ointment yet. But if you do (it's a very bright yellow), just be careful how you use it. You don't want to end up in bed like Sammy!

A Pennyworth of
Kindness

A Pennyworth of Kindness

ONCE GEORGE was on a bus going home, when a little girl got on and sat beside him. She felt in her pocket for her penny, and then she looked very scared.

She sat quite still, and George wondered what was the matter. He soon knew, when the conductor came up. George gave him his penny, and got his ticket – but the little girl began to cry.

'I must get out at the next stop,' she told the conductor. 'I must walk home. I haven't got my penny in my pocket. I must have lost it.'

'Now look here,' said the conductor, who was a cross-looking fellow, 'you're the third child who's told me that today, and . . .'

'But I really *have* lost it,' said the little girl. 'I've got a hole in my pocket.'

'Look – I can pay your fare,' said George, and he put a penny into the little girl's hand. 'My uncle gave me this penny yesterday, and you can have it.'

'Oh, thank you!' said the little girl, and she gave it to the conductor, and he handed her a ticket. 'You *are* kind. What's your name? I'll give it to you back when Mummy gives me another.'

'My name's George,' the little boy said. 'But I don't want the penny back. You can have it. I've got another one at home, and a sixpence as well.'

'All the same, I *shall* pay you back for your pennyworth of kindness,' said the little girl. That made George laugh. A pennyworth of kindness really sounded funny.

The little girl ran home to her mother, when she got out at her bus stop. She told her all about George and his kindness.

'Well, that's really nice of the boy,' said her mother. 'I wonder who he is, Mollie?'

But she couldn't find out, and Mollie never saw him on the bus again. She was worried about the penny that she hadn't paid back.

'What shall I do, Mummy?' she said. 'I must do *something* – and I've just had a birthday, so I've got lots of money.'

'Well, dear, if you can't pay the bit of kindness back to George, you can always pay it to someone else who needs it,' said her mother. 'Look out for someone.'

So Mollie looked out, and she soon found somebody. It was Mrs Forrester. Mollie saw her coming along the road, carrying a basket. Just as she came up to Mollie, the old lady slipped and fell. Her basket fell too, and there was a little crashing sound.

'Oh, dear, oh, dear!' said Mrs Forrester, picking herself up. 'There go my eggs! It's all right, little girl, I haven't hurt myself – but I've cracked my precious eggs – and I've no money to go and buy more!'

'I've got some money! I'll buy you some more, Mrs Forrester!' cried Mollie, seeing that here was a chance for her to pay the bit of kindness she owed. She raced off to the farm, explained what had happened, and bought four more eggs for a shilling. She went to Mrs Forrester's house and gave them to her.

'No, no,' said the old lady. 'I can't take them, Mollie dear. You're too kind.'

'I'm not,' said Mollie. 'I'm only paying back a pennyworth of kindness I got from a boy called George, but as I've got a lot of money just now, I've made it a shilling!'

'A shillingsworth of kindness!' said Mrs Forrester, and she laughed. 'What a funny idea – and what a good one! I owe you a shillingsworth of kindness, Mollie.'

'You don't need to pay it back to *me*, you can easily pay it to somebody else, just as I've done,' said Mollie.

Mrs Forrester quite meant to pay it back to Mollie, but she fell ill after that, and had no money to pay back anything to anyone. Her brother came to see her, and as he was both kind and well-off, he paid all her bills and took her off to his home.

'Do you owe any more money to anyone?' he asked his sister, as he put her into his car to take her away with him. 'You are sure you have told me all your bills?'

'Well – I owe a shillingsworth of kindness to a little girl,' said his sister in a feeble voice, and she told her brother about Mollie. 'I don't know where she lives – so you can't very well pay her back.'

'Well, I can pay it over to someone else instead,' said her brother. 'If you owe someone a shillingsworth of kindness I must certainly deal with it!'

He watched for a chance, but it didn't come for some time. Then he saw a little girl knocked off her bicycle by a car, and he ran to pick her up. He put her in his own car, and took her to the nearest doctor. She wasn't badly hurt, but she was very, very frightened.

The doctor soon bandaged her cut arm and leg, but Pamela still cried bitterly. 'I'll take you home now,' said Mrs Forrester's brother. 'And on the way we'll stop at a toyshop, and I'll buy you a great big doll!'

'You're very kind!' said Pamela shyly.

'Ah, I have a bit of kindness to pay to somebody,' said Mrs Forrester's brother, and he told Pamela all about how kind Mollie had been to his sister and about the penny that George had given Mollie. 'Well, here we are at the toyshop – and here's the very doll for you!'

He bought a beauty, and then drove Pamela home. He left her at the front door, and drove off, because he did not want to be thanked. Pamela went in and told her mother and father all that had happened. She showed them the beautiful doll.

'But who was this kind, generous fellow?' said her father. 'Didn't you ask his name? I must find him and pay him back his great kindness to you.'

But Pamela didn't know who had been so kind to her, and looked after her and given her the lovely doll. Her father tried his hardest to find out, but he couldn't.

Pamela was worried. 'We ought to pay back his kindness somehow, Daddy, oughtn't we?' she said. 'It all began with that pennyworth of kindness in the bus – that kind man told me the whole story – how a little boy paid a penny for a little girl's fare, and when she found she couldn't pay it back, she bought this man's sister a shillingsworth of eggs, because hers got broken – so that was a shillingsworth of kindness – and the sister couldn't pay it back because she didn't know where the little girl lived, so the brother said . . .'

'Said he'd pay it back, but to somebody else!' said her mother. She turned to Pamela's father. 'John! A pennyworth of kindness became a shillingsworth. The shillingsworth has become thirty shillingsworth, because that is what the kind fellow paid for this doll!'

'And I shall make it a hundred poundsworth!' said Pamela's father. 'My little girl is very precious to me, and I would give a hundred pounds to anyone in return for helping her. If only I could find this fellow.'

But he couldn't. So do you know what he did? He

spent his hundred pounds on buying new swings for the playground in the village, a new sandpit for the children too, and he even put in a paddling pool for the little ones.

George goes there every Saturday, with his sister Jane and his little brother Ian. Ian plays in the sandpit, Jane plays in the paddling pool, and George goes on the swings. They have a really wonderful time.

George doesn't know that all these lovely playthings were put there because of his pennyworth of kindness. He just thinks that Pamela's father must be one of the kindest men in the world to give so many marvellous things to the children in the village.

How I'd love to give someone a pennyworth of kindness and see it grow and grow! Wouldn't you? Let's try it when we get the chance.

The Astonishing Ladder

The Astonishing Ladder

BING WAS the elf who lived in Crooked Cottage in the very middle of Peeping Village. He was small and round and he was always smiling. He had plenty of money, and he kept his crooked little cottage beautifully. You should have seen how his doorknocker shone, and how his doorstep gleamed!

Most people liked Bing, he was such a cheery soul. There was only one thing against him – he was a dreadful borrower! He would keep borrowing things. He always returned them as good as new – but, you know, it was a nuisance to have your best kettle borrowed or your new spade, just when you wanted to use them yourself.

Bing borrowed brushes, baskets, chairs, tables, lamps, barrows – even ducks when he wanted the duckweed cleared off his pond! It really was very annoying of him, because he had quite enough money to buy most of the things he wanted to borrow. It was just a silly habit he had.

Now, nobody in Peeping Village liked to tell him that he was a nuisance. He was such a jolly little fellow that no one wanted to hurt his feelings. So he just went on and on borrowing things – until one day something happened.

The cottage next to his became empty, and Snip-Snap the gnome took it. He was a thin little chap with a long beard and a pointed hat on his head. Bing smiled at him over the wall, and said he was very pleased to see him.

But it wasn't long before the elf began to borrow things from Snip-Snap the gnome. First he wanted a shovel, and then he wanted the gnome's mackintosh because it was raining. Then he asked him to lend his book called *How to Keep Bees*, and then he even begged the gnome for his cat, Long-Ears, to catch the mouse that was eating the bread in his larder.

Snip-Snap lent him everything, but he didn't look too pleased about it. He didn't smile at all. He was especially annoyed about having to lend his cat, Long-Ears, because he was afraid that if Bing put the cat into his larder to catch the mouse, Long-Ears might wander into the larder another time – and eat a meat pie or something!

Well, things went on like this for some time, and Snip-Snap got very tired of it. So he spoke to Goop, the head elf of the village, and told him all about it.

'Can't you cure Bing of his terrible habit of borrowing?' he asked. 'It's true he always returns everything as good as new – but it is such a nuisance. He's always running in and out of my cottage all day long, borrowing this and borrowing that.'

'Well,' said Goop, 'it's very awkward. We don't

like to hurt Bing's feelings. He's such a good little chap. It's just a bad habit he's got into.'

'Then he ought to be cured of it,' said Snip-Snap.

'Yes, he ought to,' said Goop. 'But how? I don't know how!'

'Well, I do!' said Snip-Snap. 'I've got a good idea.'

'What is your idea?' asked Goop. But Snip-Snap shook his head.

'I don't think I'll tell you,' he said. 'You might tell someone, and if Bing got to hear of it the idea wouldn't be any good.'

'Well – it won't hurt Bing, will it?' asked Goop. 'It isn't dangerous, is it?'

'Not at all,' said Snip-Snap. 'As a matter of fact, it will be rather funny. I'll let you know when it happens, and then you can come and watch.'

'All right then,' said Goop. 'I'll come.'

Snip-Snap went home, thinking very hard. The next day he went out and bought a very good ladder. It was long enough to reach the roof of his cottage, and he left it standing there, just where Bing could see it.

That evening Snip-Snap stole out and rubbed a blue duster up and down the rungs of the ladder, murmuring a curious spell all the while. Then he went indoors to bed, and he smiled very broadly while he undressed.

Next morning Bing saw the new ladder, and he at once remembered that there was a loose tile on his roof. It would be a good idea to borrow Snip-Snap's new ladder and mend the roof. Yes, he would do that straight away.

He ran into Snip-Snap's front garden and banged loudly on the door. Snip-Snap opened it.

'I say, Snip-Snap, will you lend me your ladder today?' asked Bing. 'I've got a loose tile on my roof, and I'd like to put it right.'

'That ladder is not an ordinary one, Bing,' said Snip-Snap. 'I really wouldn't advise you to borrow it.'

'Oh, rubbish!' cried Bing brightly. 'It's a fine ladder,

and will just reach nicely to my roof. Thanks, Snip-Snap, I'll borrow it now!'

He took the ladder and carried it into his own garden. He set it up and leant it against his roof. Then he fetched a new tile, and began to climb up the ladder. Up he went and up and up.

It seemed a long way up to the roof. Bing began to pant. He looked up to see how far away the roof was, and it really didn't seem very far. So on he went again, climbing hard. But still he didn't reach the roof.

How very peculiar! Why couldn't he get to the roof? He looked down to see how far he was away from the ground – and to his enormous surprise he saw that something very strange had happened to the ladder!

As soon as he had got to the middle of the ladder, new rungs had grown! As he climbed and climbed, more and more rungs had grown, and the ladder had become curved and crooked below him, sticking out in enormous bulges to make room for the new rungs! It was really very extraordinary.

Meanwhile Snip-Snap had sent word to Goop, the head elf, to come and see what was happening. Goop came along – and when he saw Bing climbing and climbing, and more and more rungs bulging out from the ladder as he climbed, making it such a strange shape, he stood still and gaped in surprise.

The elves, pixies and gnomes who lived around all came running to see what was happening. How they stared! Then they began to laugh! It was really too funny to see Bing climbing so hard, trying to reach his roof, and only making more and more rungs behind him as he climbed – yet never getting any nearer to the roof!

Bing was upset. He saw all his friends laughing down below, and he felt hot and bothered. He went very red. He looked down at the curious ladder once more, and wondered what had happened.

'Hi, Bing! Why don't you climb down again?' called Goop. 'You'll never reach the roof at this rate.'

So Bing began to climb down – but oh, dear me, as

fast as he climbed down, more and more new rungs appeared, and soon the ladder both above and below him was full of funny bulges, twists and curves – and poor Bing got no further, either up or down!

He was frightened. The ladder was bewitched, he was sure. He remembered that Snip-Snap had warned him that it was not an ordinary ladder and had advised him not to borrow it. How silly he had been not to take his advice! Why hadn't he gone and bought a ladder for himself? He had plenty of money in his purse.

He sat down on a rung and rested. Everyone looked up at him – and how they chuckled to see such a funny sight!

'I told him not to borrow it,' said Snip-Snap, 'but he insisted. So it's his own fault.'

'Well, he will keep borrowing things,' said a pixie. 'It's a good punishment for him. Perhaps it will teach him to stop his bad habit of borrowing.'

Bing could easily hear what they said and he went very red again. Yes, it was true – he did borrow far too much. And he had no need to. It was just a bad habit he had. Well, this horrible, hateful ladder had taught him a lesson! He certainly would never, never borrow anything again in his life!

But now, what was he to do? If he climbed up, he made the ladder longer behind him – and if he climbed down, he made it longer above him. He couldn't sit still in the middle!

'I must climb down,' said Bing to himself. 'I shall have to climb over all those bulges and twists, but it can't be helped. It's only by going that way that I shall get anywhere at all!'

So he began to climb down. Oh my goodness, it was difficult, and such a long way to climb too! There were hundreds of rungs to put his feet on, one after another, and Bing soon began to puff and pant again.

By this time the whole village of Peeping was gathered outside Bing's cottage, watching him. They thought it was the funniest sight they had seen for a long time. How they chuckled and laughed!

At last Bing reached the ground. He stepped off the last rung and sat panting on the grass. Then Snip-Snap walked up to him and spoke solemnly.

'Can I have my ladder back, Bing? I want to use it myself.'

'You can take it back with pleasure,' said Bing. 'It's a nasty, horrible ladder, bewitched and enchanted, and I don't want to have any more to do with it. I wish I hadn't borrowed it – and what's more, I'll never in my life borrow anything again! The ladder's taught me a lesson!'

'Well, I'll take it away now,' said Snip-Snap. 'I want to put a new tile on my chimney.'

'You don't mean to say you're going to climb up that awful ladder?' cried Bing in surprise. 'Don't do it, Snip-Snap, I beg of you! It will play you tricks just as it did me, and you'll be sorry.'

'I'm not afraid,' said Snip-Snap. He picked up the twisted ladder and carried it into his own garden – and as he went he whispered the spell that took away the enchantment from the ladder – and it gradually shortened itself until at last, just as he put it against his roof, it was a proper ladder again, short and straight.

'Now, why has it gone straight, I wonder?' said Bing, getting to his feet in surprise.

'It doesn't like being borrowed,' Snip-Snap said solemnly. 'Well, I'm going up to see to my chimney. Goodbye, Bing, I should go in and have a rest – and then, if I were you, I should take your money and go out to buy all the things you have thought of borrowing this week. It would be safer!'

Bing went indoors and sat down in his armchair. He made himself a hot cup of cocoa, and nibbled a ginger biscuit, thinking very hard. And in the end he took Snip-Snap's advice – he went out and bought all the things he had ever borrowed, or had thought of borrowing! Kettles, saucepans, spades, lamps, ducks – and even a cat and a dog!

Now he feels safe – and since that day when he

climbed up that astonishing ladder he has never, never borrowed anything at all from anybody – no, not even a pin!

The Impossible Wish

The Impossible Wish

ONCE UPON a time Twinks, the magical brownie, when he was digging in his garden, came upon an old iron box. He hoped there might be treasure inside, but, stars and moon, when he opened it, out came a long, smoky wizard! He had been put into the box because of some mischief he had done – and now he was free again!

'I will grant you a hundred wishes a day!' said the wizard gratefully to the scared brownie.

'Oh, thank you very much!' said Twinks, delighted. 'I'd like a treacle pudding to begin with. That will save me cooking my dinner.'

The treacle pudding appeared in a dish. Twinks wasn't long in finishing it. The wizard waited. Then he spoke again. 'Your next wish, please? Remember, brownie, you must wish one hundred wishes a day. Hurry, please!'

'What would happen if I couldn't think of a hundred wishes?' asked Twinks.

'Oh, you would be my servant then,' said the wizard with a grin. 'Come, think of some more.'

Well, Twinks thought of a castle with a hundred windows, a suit of gold and silver, a black horse with blue eyes, six dogs all alike, some fried bacon and eggs, a box of peppermints and heaps of other things. He managed to get his hundred wishes in, but he had to hurry himself!

Before a week had gone by Twinks had every single thing he had ever wanted, and he was finding it very hard indeed to think of any more wishes. Whatever was he to do?

'I wish I could think of something you couldn't

get,' he groaned to the wizard.

'That is impossible,' said the wizard. 'If you could think of that, then I would go away and you would never see me again!'

Now Twinks remembered a small boy who was very sharp indeed, and he wondered if he could help him. He went to find him, and soon he had told Donald his trouble. The little boy grinned and nodded. 'Yes, I'll help you,' he said. 'Take me back to your castle.' So back they went, and very soon the wizard appeared to hear Twinks's daily batch of wishes.

'Grant my friend's wishes,' said Twinks, waving his hand towards Donald.

'I want a nice hot ice cream,' said Donald at once. 'I love ice creams – but the weather is so cold that it sets my teeth on edge if the ice cream is too cold. Get me a hot one, please.'

The wizard bowed, reached his hand into the air, and produced a dish on which an ice cream stood. He popped the dish on the kitchen stove – and immediately the ice cream melted and became hot custard. The wizard put it in front of Donald.

'Don't be silly, wizard,' said Donald, pushing away the plate. 'This is only hot custard. Taste it.'

'So it is,' said the wizard. He took another ice cream from the air and heated that too – but of course it melted again into creamy custard! Again and again the puzzled wizard tried to give Donald hot ice cream – it was quite impossible!

'I cannot do it!' he cried, and straight away he became smoky, streamed up the chimney and vanished. And from that day to this no one has ever heard of him. But if he *should* appear again, you'll know what to ask him for, won't you!

The House Made
of Cards

The House Made
of Cards

WENDY AND Jack had built a lovely house out of their playing cards. First they put two leaning together, then they put two more on each side, then they put two on top of the side ones resting on them, and built another room on top of that. You know how to do it, don't you?

They made such a big house! Really, they had never made such a large card house before! It was a perfectly lovely one. Wendy called their mother and she cried out in surprise.

'Well, you certainly have built a fine house this time!' she said.

'Could we leave it on the table till the morning?' asked Jack. 'It seems a shame to knock it down tonight.'

'Well, leave it there,' said Mother. 'You can see it tomorrow then. I won't touch it when I lay the table for breakfast.'

So the two children left their card house on the table. How big it was!

That night, when all was dark in the room except for the moonlight shining in at the window, a small pixie came hurrying out of a mouse hole where he had been hiding.

He was looking for a house to live in. He looked into the doll's house, but the dolls wouldn't let him in.

'We know you, Mr Grabby!' they said. 'You'd take the best bed to sleep in, the most comfortable chair to sit in and the nicest cake out of the oven! No, thank you! We don't want you here. Go and look for somewhere else to live!'

Mr Grabby, the pixie, made a rude face at the dolls and wandered off. Then he suddenly saw the lovely house of cards on the table!

'My,' he said, 'that's a fine house! I wonder if anyone lives there? If nobody does, I shall live there myself! Shan't I be grand! I wonder how many rooms it has?'

He walked into the house of cards. Dear me, it had ten rooms! Would you believe it? Grabby was delighted. He had never had such a grand house before.

He took his tiny magic wand and waved it. He meant to make chairs, tables and beds by magic, and he was just going to utter the right words when he heard a little voice calling to him.

'Mr Grabby! Is this your house?'

Grabby looked out of the top room to see who was speaking. It was the little mouse in whose hole he had been hiding all day.

'Yes, this is my house!' he said grandly. 'What do you want?'

'Well, Mr Grabby, that old black cat has come into the house tonight and she's sitting near my hole,' said the mouse. 'I daren't go back there. So I thought you would perhaps give me shelter in your grand house for tonight.'

'I can't,' said the selfish pixie. 'I want all the rooms myself. I don't want any mice here.'

'Oh, Mr Grabby,' said the tiny mouse, 'how unkind of you! Didn't I share my hole with you when you asked me to yesterday? Please share your house with me till the cat goes away.'

'I tell you I won't!' said Grabby crossly. 'Go away and be eaten! You're a nuisance!'

Now that made the mouse feel very angry indeed. He made up his mind that he would sleep in the house of cards that night. So he crept in at the bottom of it and lay down to sleep. But the pixie knew he was there and came flying down in a rage. He hit at the mouse with his wand.

'Ow!' cried the mouse and climbed quickly into the room above. The pixie flew after him. Up went the mouse and scrambled into another room. The pixie followed, shouting out in a dreadful temper.

The pixie tried to hit out at the mouse whenever he could. Soon the tiny creature thought that the pixie was the horridest fellow he had ever met.

'I wish I hadn't shared my hole with you!' he squeaked as he ran in and out of one room after another. 'I wish I hadn't! I wish I hadn't!'

Poor little mouse! The pixie caught him at last and hit him on the nose with his magic wand. The little mouse wept tears all down the cards. Then he crept away to the very end of the table and washed his face, thinking hard all the time.

'That pixie wants punishing!' said the mouse. 'He's selfish and unkind. I share things with others so why shouldn't he? I shall punish him!'

He watched the pixie climb up into the topmost room of the house of cards. He saw him take a handkerchief out of his pocket to polish up his magic wand.

'I shall go and nibble his house away at the bottom!' said the mouse to himself. 'Yes, that's what I will do!'

So, as soon as the pixie had forgotten all about him, he crept back to the house and began to nibble at a card. How he nibbled with his sharp little teeth!

Soon the card was gnawed almost through. It dropped flat on to the table, for it could no longer stand upright! And as soon as it dropped, all the house of cards came tumbling down!

Flip, flap, flip, flap! Down it came and the cards swished softly into a heap on the table. There was no house left. How astonished that pixie was! He had tumbled down with the cards, and bumped his head.

'Oh, oh!' he cried in a fright. 'What is happening? It's an earthquake, it's an earthquake! I must fly away quickly!'

He spread his wings and flew away, quite forgetting to take his little magic wand with him. It lay under the cards. The mouse didn't see it either. He chuckled to himself when he saw what a fright the pixie was in.

'Serves him right!' he said. 'And see! The noise of

the cards falling has frightened away the cat! I can go back to my hole in safety!'

Back he went, and all was quiet in the room until the children came in the next morning.

'Oh, look!' cried Jack. 'Our lovely house of cards has fallen down. And what is this? A card nibbled quite in half! A mouse must have done that – but I wonder why?'

Wendy picked up the cards – and suddenly she found the tiny magic wand.

'Look at this,' she said to Jack. 'What is it? It looks like a thin silver matchstick with a star at the end!'

'Ooh, it's a magic wand!' said Jack. 'Let's use it and see what happens!'

But before they could wish anything their mother called them to go and get ready for school. Wasn't it a pity?

'Never mind, we'll use it tonight after tea!' said Wendy. I do wish I was going to be there, don't you?

The Salt, Salt Sea

The Salt, Salt Sea

ONCE UPON a time there lived a king who ruled over a small island in the midst of the sea.

Now, although the island was bare and poor, the king was rich. Princes, lords and kings came from the mainland to see him, and each brought with him gold and precious jewels. In return for these the king of the island gave them a sack of white salt!

In those days salt was rarer and more precious than rubies. The poor people could never buy even a pinch, and kings and princes were willing to pay much gold for enough salt to last them one year. On the island were salt-mines and from these the king made his money.

Now, one day a fisherman by the shore found a curious yellow jar washed up by the tide. It was round and squat and had a small opening at the top. The fisherman picked it up and took it home to his wife. She cleaned it and filled it full of vinegar, which she placed on the table for her husband to use with his onions. Imagine her surprise when she found that it was always full! No matter how much she tilted it to use the vinegar, it was never empty! It continually ran with vinegar!

'It is enchanted, husband!' cried the woman. They filled it with all sorts of things, but no matter what it was filled with, it ran with that for hours, as soon as it was tilted. Then the fisherman was struck with an idea and leapt to his feet.

'Wife!' he said. 'We will get some salt and fill this strange jar. Then we will go to the mainland in my boat and sell cheaply to the kings and princes. We shall make much money and be rich in no time! This jar will go on pouring out salt as long as we wish!'

So that night the fisherman went to the silent salt-mines and stole enough salt to fill his yellow jar. Then back to his boat he went and set his sail to go away. In his trembling hand he held the salt-filled jar, and every time he tilted it the white salt poured out in a never-ending stream.

But, as he sped over the dark night waters, big clouds blew up from the west, and thunder rolled. The lightning streaked the sky, and a great wind took hold of the little ship and bent it almost to the water. The fisherman sprang to take down his sail, and dropped the yellow jar in his haste, thinking to pick it up later. The wind blew him back to the shore, and he dared not set out again that night. He searched for the yellow jar but it was not to be found! 'It has rolled overboard!' said the fisherman mournfully. 'We shall never be rich now!'

He was right. The strange jar had rolled into the sea, and had fallen upside down between two rocks. There it lay, pouring out salt all night through.

And, as no one has ever moved it since, it has poured out salt all through the years, until now all the seas are as salty as can be! I'd like to find that yellow jar. Wouldn't you?

The Goblin in the Train

The Goblin in the Train

ALL THE toys in the playroom were most excited. Tomorrow the clockwork train was going to take them to a pixie party, and what fun that would be.

But, oh, dear, wasn't it a shame, when Andrew was playing with the train that day, he overwound it and broke the spring. Then it wouldn't go, and all the toys crowded round it that night, wondering what they would do the next night when they wanted to go to the party.

'I'm very sorry,' said the clockwork train. 'But I simply can't move a wheel, you know. My spring is quite broken. You won't be able to go to the pixie party, because I can't take you. It's all Andrew's fault.'

'Well, he must have broken your spring by accident,' said the ragdoll. 'He's very careful with us, generally. But it is dreadfully disappointing.'

'Couldn't we send a message to the little goblin who lives under the holly bush?' said the teddy bear. 'He is very clever at mending things, and he might be able to mend the broken spring.'

'Good idea!' cried the toys, and they at once sent a message to the goblin. He came in five minutes, and shook his head when he saw the broken spring.

'This will take me a long time to mend,' he said. 'I doubt if I'll get it done by cock-crow.'

'Please, please try!' cried the toys. So he set to work. He had all sorts of weird tools, not a bit like ours, and he worked away as hard as ever he could. And suddenly, just as he had almost finished, a cock crowed! That meant that all toys and fairy folk must scuttle away to their own places again, but the goblin couldn't bear to leave his job unfinished.

'I'll just pop into the cab of the train,' he called to the toys. 'I'll make myself look like a little driver, and as Andrew knows the spring is broken, perhaps he won't look at the train today or notice me. Then I can quickly finish my work tonight and you'll be able to go to the party!'

The toys raced off to their cupboard, thinking how very kind the goblin was. He hopped into the cab, sat down there, and kept quite still, just as if he were a little boy driver.

Andrew didn't once look at his engine that day, and the toys were so glad. When night came again the goblin set to work, and very soon he had finished mending the spring. He wound up the engine, and hey presto, its wheels went round and it raced madly round the playroom.

'Good! Good!' cried the toys. 'Now we can go to the party! Hurrah! What can we do to return your kindness, goblin?'

'Well,' said the goblin, turning rather red, 'there is

one thing I'd like. You know, I've never been asked to a pixie party in my life. I suppose you wouldn't take me with you? If you could, I'd drive the train, and see that nothing went wrong with it.'

'Of course, of course!' shouted the toys in glee. 'You shall come with us, goblin, and we'll tell the pixies how nice you are!'

Then they all got into the train, the goblin wound it up again, and they went to the party. What a glorious time they had, and what a hero the goblin was when the toys had finished telling everyone how he had mended the broken train!

He drove them all safely back again to the playroom and then, guess what, he was so happy and so tired that he fell fast asleep sitting in the cab!

And in the morning Andrew found him there and was so surprised.

'Look, Mummy, look!' he shouted. 'The train has suddenly got a driver, and gosh, the spring is mended too! Isn't that a strange thing, and isn't he a nice little driver! Wherever could he have come from?'

But his mother couldn't think how he could have got there.

'He must have been there all the time and you didn't notice him before,' she said.

'No, Mummy, really,' said Andrew. 'I've often wished my clockwork train had a driver, and I know I should have noticed him if he had been here before. Oh, I do hope he stays. He looks so nice and real.'

The goblin was so happy to find that Andrew liked him and was pleased with him. But he was happier still that night when all the toys crowded round him and begged him to stay and be one of them.

'We like you very much,' they said. 'Don't go back to your holly bush, but stay here and be the driver of Andrew's train. We'll have such fun together every night!'

The goblin wanted nothing better than to stay where he was, for he had often been very lonely under his holly bush.

'I'd love to stay!' he said. 'Come on, I'll take you for a fine ride round and round the playroom!' The toys almost woke Andrew up with their shouts of delight.

Andrew is very proud of his train driver. He shows him to everyone, and I do hope you'll see him for yourself some day. Then perhaps you can tell Andrew the story of how he got there.

The Box of Magic

The Box of Magic

ONCE UPON a time, when Muddle and Twink, the two elves, were walking along over Bumble Bee Common, they found a strange box lying on the path. Muddle picked it up and opened it.

'Twink!' he cried in amazement. 'Look! It's full of wishing feathers!'

Twink looked and whistled in surprise. 'Jumping buttons!' he said. 'What a find! I say, Muddle, we'll have the time of our lives now, wishing all we want to! Come on – let's hurry home, shall we, and do a bit of wishing?'

Neither of the two naughty elves thought that what

they really ought to do was to find out who the box of wishing feathers belonged to. No, they simply scurried to their cottage as fast as ever they could, Muddle carrying the box under his arm.

They ran in at their little front door, and put the box on the table. They took off the lid and there lay the wishing feathers, dozens of them. Do you know what a wishing feather is like? It is pink at the bottom, green in the middle and bright shining silver at the tip – and it smells of cherry pie, so you will always know one by that!

Well, there lay the pink, green and silver feathers, all smelling most deliciously of cherry pie. Twink and Muddle gazed at them in delight. Twink picked up a feather.

'I wish for a fine hot treacle pudding!' he cried, waving his feather. It at once flew out of the window and in came a large dish with a steaming hot treacle pudding on it. Unfortunately Muddle was in the way and it bumped into his head. The pudding fell off the dish and the hot treacle went down Muddle's neck. Crash! The dish broke on the floor.

'Ooh! Ah! Ooh!' wept Muddle.

'You silly creature!' cried Twink in a rage, as he saw his beautiful pudding on the floor. 'What do you want to get in the way for? Just like you, Muddle, always muddling everything!'

'You nasty, unkind thing!' said Muddle fiercely. 'Why didn't you tell me you were going to wish for a silly pudding like this? Ooh! I wish the treacle was all down your neck instead of mine, that's what I wish!'

A wishing feather flew from the box and out of the window as Muddle said this, and the treacle down his neck vanished – and appeared all round poor Twink's neck! How he yelled.

'I hate you!' he shouted at Muddle, trying to wipe away the treacle. 'I wish you were a frog and had a duck after you!'

A wishing feather flew out of the window once

more – and, my goodness me, Muddle disappeared and in his place came a large green frog, who shouted angrily in Muddle's voice. Just behind him appeared a big white duck, saying 'Quack, quack' in excitement as she saw the frog.

Then hoppity-hop went Muddle all round the room, trying to escape the duck. Twink laughed till the tears ran down his face and mixed with the treacle!

'Oh, you wicked rogue!' shouted froggy Muddle. 'I wish you were a canary with a cat after you!'

Oh, dear! Immediately poor Twink disappeared and in his place appeared a bright yellow canary, rather larger than an ordinary one. Just behind came a big tabby cat saying 'Mew, mew!' excitedly at the sight of the canary. Then what a to-do there was! Muddle, still a frog, was trying to escape the duck, and Twink, a canary, was trying to fly away from the pouncing cat. Neither of the two had any breath for wishes, and what would have happened to them goodness knows – if the cat hadn't suddenly seen the duck!

'Miaow!' it said and pounced after the waddling duck. With a quack of fright the white bird waddled out of the cottage, the cat after her. As soon as they went out of the door, they disappeared into smoke. It was most strange.

The frog and the canary looked at one another. They felt rather ashamed of themselves.

'I wish we were both our ordinary selves again,' said Muddle in rather a small voice. At once the frog and the canary disappeared and the two elves stood looking at one another.

'This sort of thing won't do,' said Twink. 'We shall waste all the wishing feathers if we do things like this, you know, Muddle.'

'Well, let's wish for something sensible now,' said Muddle. 'What about wishing for a nice, big, friendly dog, Twink? We've always wanted a dog, you know. Now is our chance.'

'All right,' said Twink. 'Let's wish for a black and white one, shall we?'

'No, I'd rather it was a brown and white one,' said Muddle. 'I like that kind best.'

'Well, I prefer a black and white one,' said Twink. 'I wish for a black and white dog!'

Immediately a large black and white dog appeared, and wagged its tail at the elves.

'I wish you to be brown and white!' said Muddle at once, scowling at his friend. The dog obligingly changed its colour from black to brown. Twink was furious. 'I wish you to be black and white!' he yelled. The dog changed again, looking rather astonished.

'Now, don't let's be silly,' said Muddle, trying to keep his temper. 'I tell you, Twink, a dog is nicer if it is brown and white. I wish it to be . . .'

'Stop!' said Twink fiercely. 'It's my dog! I won't have you changing its colour like this! Wish for a dog of your own if you want to, but don't keep interfering with mine.'

'I wish for a brown and white dog!' said Muddle at once. A large brown and white dog immediately walked in at the door, wagging its tail in a most friendly fashion. But as soon as the black and white one saw it, it began to growl very fiercely and showed its teeth.

'Grr!' it said.

'Grrr!' the other dog said back. The black and white dog then flew at the other.

'Call off your horrid dog!' yelled Muddle to Twink. 'It's trying to bite mine! Oh! Oh! Look at it!'

'Well, you should have been content with one dog,' said Twink. 'You see, my dog thinks this is its home, and it won't let a strange dog come in. Quite right, too. It's a good dog!'

'It isn't, it isn't!' cried Muddle. 'Oh, dear, oh, dear, do call off your dog, Twink. Look, it's trying to bite the tail of mine.'

'Of course it is,' said Twink. 'I tell you, mine is a very good dog. Tell your dog to go away, then it won't get hurt.'

'Why should I?' shouted Muddle in a temper again.

'My dog has as much right as yours to be here. Isn't this my home as much as yours? Then my dog can live here if I say so! Oh, look, look, your dog has bitten my dog's collar in half!'

Muddle was in such a rage that he ran to Twink's dog, his hand raised as if to smack it. The dog at once turned round, growled and tried to bite Muddle, who jumped away and ran round the room. The dog, thinking it was a game, ran after him, and Muddle was very much frightened.

'Call him off, call him off!' he yelled. But Twink sat down on the sofa and laughed till the tears ran down his long nose. He thought it was a funny sight to see Muddle being chased by his dog.

'I wish my dog would go and bite you, you horrid thing!' yelled Muddle. Then it was Twink's turn to jump up and run – for the brown and white dog ran at Twink, showing all its white teeth.

Twink ran out of the cottage followed by a snapping dog, and Muddle ran out too, the other dog trying to nip his leg.

'Oh!' cried Twink, as he was bitten on the hand.

'Ooh!' yelled Muddle, as he was nipped in the leg. 'I wish the dogs weren't here any more! I wish we hadn't got those horrid wishing feathers that seem to make things go all wrong!'

In a trice the two dogs vanished and the box of feathers sailed away through the air, back to the Green Wizard who had lost them that morning. The two elves stood looking at one another, Twink holding his hand and Muddle holding his leg.

'The dogs have gone but they've left their bites behind them,' groaned Twink. 'Why didn't you wish those away too, Muddle? The feathers have gone now, so we can't do any more wishing.'

'Well, our wishing didn't do us any good, did it?' said Muddle. 'Come on in, Twink, and let us bathe our bites. We have behaved badly and we deserve our punishment. My goodness, if I find wishing feathers again, I'll be more sensible. Won't you?'

'Rather!' said Twink, holding his sore hand. But I don't expect they ever will find such a thing again, do you?

The Unlucky Little Boy

The Unlucky Little Boy

THERE WAS once a boy called Kenneth who was most unlucky. If anyone lost anything it was always Kenneth. If someone fell down and hurt his knee, it was sure to be Kenneth. Really, he was most unfortunate!

He was a kind boy too, always willing to run errands, or lend his toys or clear up for his mother. He certainly didn't deserve to be unlucky – but some people just seem to be, don't they!

One day he was rushing home from school to meet his Uncle Fred, who was going to take him out on his motorbike after tea. Just as he ran across the field his foot caught against a stone – and down he fell, bang! 'Bother!' said Kenneth. 'Just my luck when I'm in a hurry!'

He had fallen into a ditch, and as he got up he saw two frightened eyes staring at him. Kenneth stared back – and no wonder, for it was a magical brownie that was looking at him! The little boy had never in his life seen a fairy before, and he was too much surprised to say a word.

'It's too bad of you,' said the brownie at last, in a voice like a squirrel's. 'You've fallen on my house – and crushed it to bits – just as I was giving a party this afternoon! I think you ought to mend it for me.'

Kenneth saw that he had fallen on to a quaint little house made of foxgloves tied together and hung with curtains of spider webs.

'I say, I *am* sorry!' he said. 'I would stay and put it right for you, but I'm hurrying home to have a treat.'

'Oh,' said the brownie, and looked so unhappy that Kenneth changed his mind. 'All right!' he said. 'I'll do what I can, even if I have to miss my Uncle Fred.'

So with neat, careful fingers he pulled the foxgloves straight, tied a stick to a broken one, and hung a bit of moss down one side of the tiny house, where the spider web had quite broken. It took a long time.

'Oh, thank you!' said the brownie gratefully. 'I do hope this hasn't meant that you will miss your treat.'

'I expect it does mean that,' said Kenneth. 'I am very unlucky, you know. I wish I was lucky! But I always seem to miss the nice things and come in for the nasty ones!'

'You don't deserve that,' said the brownie. 'You are a kind boy, and deserve to have *good* things happen to you. I think I can help you. Look carefully in the dark green patch on your lawn this evening and see what you can find!'

Kenneth ran off, puzzled. Sure enough, his Uncle Fred had gone without waiting for him – another treat spoilt. The little boy was disappointed. He went out to look on his lawn to see what he could find. He saw a dark patch of clover leaves, and knelt down by it.

But hunt as he might he could not find anything hidden there to help him.

And then he suddenly did! What did he find, children? Yes – he found a four-leaved clover among all the hundreds of three-leaved ones! A four-leaved clover! That is one of the luckiest things in the world!

And will you believe it, Kenneth isn't unlucky any longer. He gets treats now like anyone else. And as he is kind, he sometimes lends his precious clover-leaf to anyone with bad luck, just to help them. Do try and find one yourself, just to see what happens!

The Little Silver Hat

The Little Silver Hat

ONCE UPON a time there was a fairy called Silver-Wings. As you can guess, she had wings of silver, and her dress shone like silver too. She wore silvery shoes, and was the merriest little thing imaginable.

She badly wanted a silver cap, but she couldn't get one anywhere. She tried in all the hat shops she knew, but not one of them had a silver cap.

'We don't make silver caps,' everyone said. 'They would be too expensive!'

So Silver-Wings had to go without a silver cap and she was very sad about it.

And then one day she found one! It was such a

surprise. She had been watching a little girl sitting sewing among the buttercups, and thinking what a good little girl she was. The child was making a dress for her doll and was doing it as carefully as she could. In and out flew her needle, in and out.

The church clock struck eleven, and the little girl put down her work. 'Time for a break,' she said, and she took three biscuits out of a bag. She began to munch them, and the fairy crept nearer to look at the dress that the little girl was making.

And there, just by the little girl's sewing, was a silver hat! It was tall and shiny and silvery, and it shone in the sun.

Silver-Wings snatched it up in joy. She tried it on her head and it fitted perfectly! She ran to the nearest pool and looked at herself. She was as pretty as a picture!

Joyfully she danced through the buttercups and daisies, showing her new silver hat to the beetles and the butterflies, the ladybirds and the bees. They thought it was simply lovely.

'It's just what you wanted!' said a butterfly.

'It does suit you!' hummed a bee.

'Wherever did you find it?' cried a beetle.

'In this field!' said the fairy. 'Just by that little girl over there.'

A bee flew over to have a look at the little girl. He flew back again. 'There is something the matter with that little girl,' he hummed. 'She looked worried.'

The fairy flew off to see what was the matter. The little girl was certainly looking worried. She was hunting all over the place for something.

'I can't possibly get on with my work unless I find it!' Silver-Wings heard her say. 'Oh, dear, oh, dear, wherever can it have gone?'

The fairy was sorry to hear that the little girl had lost something she wanted. She suddenly flew down beside the child and spoke to her in her high little voice.

'Can I help you? What have you lost?'

'I've lost my thimble,' said the little girl. 'The thing

I put on my finger to stop the end of the needle from hurting it when I stitch.'

The little girl looked at the fairy as she spoke and then stared in surprise.

'What's the matter?' asked the fairy. 'Do you like my new hat?'

'Well,' said the little girl, 'you may think it's a hat, Fairy – but I think it's my thimble!'

And so it was! The fairy had picked up the little girl's thimble and had taken it for a hat! Would you believe it!

They stared at one another. Then the little girl began to laugh. How she laughed!

'Fancy using my thimble for a hat!' she cried. 'But oh, it does fit you so beautifully and you look so sweet in it! It's just what you wanted!'

'Yes, isn't it?' said the fairy, taking it off sadly. 'I'm sorry I took it, though, and made you hunt for it. Here it is.'

'Now listen, fairy,' said the little girl. 'I will finish

my doll's dress and use my thimble till lunchtime. Then I will go home – but I will give you my silver thimble for a hat! I have another thimble at home, so I can spare you this one!'

Wasn't it nice of her? The fairy sat beside the little girl for the rest of the morning and watched her sewing quickly and neatly, with the silver thimble on her middle finger – and then, when the church clock struck one, the little girl folded up her work, and gave the fairy her thimble.

'There you are!' she said. 'You may have it! Come and peep at me sometimes and let me see how nice you look in your thimble hat!'

So now Silver-Wings has a silver hat – though, if ever you see her, you will know at once that it is only somebody's little thimble!

The Toys' New Palace

The Toys' New Palace

JACK AND Tilly had built a palace with their bricks. It was a very good one – very tall and grand, with windows and a door and lots of towers and turrets. The children were pleased with it.

'It's a pity nobody ever lives in the houses and palaces we build,' said Tilly. 'They are just wasted, really. We build them, and then we knock them down.'

'I wish we didn't have to knock this palace down,' said Jack, looking at it proudly. 'It really is one of the best we've ever made, don't you think? Look, Mummy! Don't you think our palace is good?'

'Splendid!' said Mother. 'But now it's time for bed

so you must put your bricks away.'

'Couldn't we leave this palace up for just one night?' said Tilly longingly. 'It's such a fine palace after all and it has taken us all day to build. It would be so nice to lie in bed and think of it standing here in the moonlight, looking so real.'

'We could imagine that the fairies had arrived and were having a grand feast inside it,' added Jack. 'Wouldn't that be fun!'

'Well, you can leave it till the morning if you want to,' said Mother. 'But now you must hurry off to bed. It's past your bedtime already.'

Little did the children realise that, as soon as they had left the room, their toys all started to come to life. The big teddy bear let all the toys out of the toy cupboard. The dolls woke up inside the doll's house. All the animals on the toy farm came awake and the clockwork train started running about all over the floor.

It happened every night and this night the toys

were pleased to find that the children had left them a splendid palace to play in. They thought it was a very fine present indeed!

When the children were safely in bed, and the room was in darkness except for the big silver moon shining through the window, the big teddy bear ran right across the floor and looked through the doorway of the fine wooden palace.

'I say! It's the best thing that ever was!' he called. 'Come on, toys! Look what the children have built for us! See this window – and that one – and look at the turrets and spires at the top. My, haven't they built it well!'

'It's splendid!' said one of the doll's house dolls. 'Can we go inside?'

Just then there came a loud banging noise from just above them. It was someone knocking on the window.

'Come in!' called the teddy bear, surprised that anyone could come calling so late at night. And he was even more surprised when a large grey mouse appeared on the windowsill, wearing a postman's cap on his head. He carried a letter in his hand and was busy looking all around the room for someone particular to deliver it to.

'Does the clockwork mouse live here?' he asked.

'Oh, yes!' squeaked the little mouse in astonishment, and he ran over to the postman. 'Here I am!'

'I have a letter for you from the king of the mice,' said the postman in an important voice, handing it over.

Then he turned on his tail and was gone again. The toys heard him pattering away along the garden path. The clockwork mouse stared at his letter in surprise. Then he tore it open.

'Oh!' he said excitedly. 'Oh! Listen to this – the king and queen of the mice are coming to visit! They are on their way to Mouseland, and they have decided to stay here for the night! They ask if they can be my guests! Oh, what an honour it is to be sure!'

The clockwork mouse was so excited that he ran up and down the room without stopping. Up and down he went, until his clockwork ran down and the teddy had to wind him up again.

'There is only one problem,' said the mouse when he had calmed down. 'The toy cupboard is all very well, but it would be so much nicer if I had a special place where the king and queen could stay. I've only my old box for them to sleep in, and nothing at all to offer them to eat. Oh, dear, I wish I could think of something better! What shall I do? Fancy the king and queen coming to stay here! I can't get over the surprise!'

'Don't worry, clockwork mouse,' said the big teddy bear, patting him on the back. 'I have just had a wonderful idea. We can give the king and queen of the mice a splendid welcome. They can spend the night in a palace – the palace of bricks! It's just the right size for them! And as a special treat I will hide behind the coal scuttle with the musical box and turn the handle so that it plays music for them when they arrive.'

'And I know where Jack dropped half his biscuit

this morning,' said the curly-haired doll excitedly. 'It rolled into the corner of the floor over there!'

'And there are two sweets left in the toy sweetshop. I saw them there this afternoon!' said Panda. 'Oh, clockwork mouse, you don't need to be worried – we will help you to welcome the king and queen of the mice. They are sure to have a lovely time!'

Well, you should have seen how those toys rushed about to get things ready!

First they took all the furniture and the tiny rugs from the old doll's house and put them into the palace of bricks. They found blankets and pillows for the tiny beds to make them comfortable. Then two of the ragdolls leant out of the big window and picked some flowers to put on the table.

The teddy bear found a little toy lantern and managed to hang it from the ceiling of the palace. He switched it on. How lovely the palace of bricks looked with the light shining inside!

The curly-haired doll found the bit of biscuit and

put it on a tiny plate on the table. Meanwhile Panda and the toy dog carried the sweet bottle out of the toy sweetshop and arranged the sweets on the table too. Just then there was a shout from the clockwork mouse. He had found half a cup of lemonade that the children had left. It would make a fine drink for the king and queen.

Then the teddy bear hid behind the coal scuttle with the musical box. He began to turn the handle! The music sounded so lovely – everything was ready!

Just then, out from a hole in the floorboards came the king and queen of the mice! They had tiny crowns on their heads, and looked rather funny – but, dear me, they were the king and queen all right! Twenty small mice followed them, blowing on twenty golden trumpets as they came.

The clockwork mouse, with a new blue bow round his neck, ran to welcome them all. Then he proudly led them to the palace of bricks, bowing politely. The king and queen were amazed and delighted.

'What a fine place you have here, clockwork mouse!' said the king.

'And what lovely music!' said the queen, looking all round for the band. But of course she didn't see the teddy bear hiding behind the coal scuttle, turning the musical box handle as fast as he could!

'And you've provided a feast too!' said the king, beginning to nibble the biscuit. 'Very nice, clockwork mouse, very nice indeed.'

'Look at these lovely sweets!' said the queen mouse, tasting one. 'This surely must be one of the nicest places we have ever visited. It is most kind of you, little mouse.'

After they had eaten, the king and queen had a fine dance all around the palace and invited the toys to join in. Soon the whole room was filled with dancing figures and the poor teddy bear played the musical box till his arm nearly fell off.

In the middle of it all Jack and Tilly heard the musical box playing and came to see what was going on!

How they stared when they saw what was happening!

Their palace of bricks shone like gold in the light of the toy lantern. And all over the floor there were toys and mice playing and dancing to the sound of sweet music.

But as soon as the toys saw the two children they scampered inside the palace and hid. Jack and Tilly thought they must have imagined the whole thing and went to bed.

When the first light of morning began to shine through the window it was time for the king and queen to leave for Mouseland.

'Goodbye, clockwork mouse! Goodbye, toys!' they squeaked as they disappeared through the hole in the floorboards. 'We'll send you an invitation to our palace one day!' they said, and the next minute they had gone.

Later that morning the children came to play in the room. The palace of bricks looked quite ordinary in the daylight and Jack and Tilly were disappointed to think that what they had seen had been nothing but a dream.

But can you guess what happened? Why, the toys had forgotten to take out the chairs and tables and the lantern.

'Goodness me!' exclaimed Jack. 'So we did see something after all!'

'We wanted someone to live in our palace, and they did!' said Tilly in delight.

As for the clockwork mouse, he is very happy now, for any day he is expecting an invitation from the king of the mice to go and stay with him at his palace in Mouseland. I hope it comes soon, don't you?

Blackberry Magic

Blackberry Magic

ONCE UPON a time there were twin boys called Joe and Jim. They were very alike in their looks, but that was all. In everything else they were as different as different could be.

Joe was cheery and bright, and would do anything for anybody. Jim was bad-tempered, and was the sort of boy who wants to be paid for doing anything. He wouldn't go on an errand, or lay the table or dig the garden, unless his mother promised him some money.

So now you know them both.

It happened one day that their mother wanted to

make some blackberry jam and so she called her boys in.

'Will you go and pick me some blackberries out in the fields?' she asked.

'Of course we will, Mum,' answered Joe, picking up a basket. 'Come on, Jim.'

'Oh, bother!' said Jim. 'I was playing a game!'

'Well, so was Joe!' said his mother. 'Run along now!'

'Mum, will you give me some money if I go?' asked Jim sulkily. He hated doing a job if he didn't get any money for it.

'No, I won't,' his mother said sharply. 'You are always asking for money and you always spend it on yourself. I'm going to make the blackberries into jam for you, and that ought to be quite enough reward. You're a selfish little boy!'

'I don't want to go and pick blackberries then,' said Jim.

'Very well,' said his mother, and went indoors, sadly wondering what she could do to stop Jim's selfishness.

Joe went whistling off by himself, carrying two baskets, for he meant to fill them both for his mother, as Jim wouldn't come. He soon arrived at the bramble-spread hedgerow in the lane, where the blackberries grew black and juicy in hundreds and thousands.

Joe picked quickly, wondering if he could fill the two baskets before the sun started to go down. He had nearly filled one when he saw a little man, dressed in red and brown, come hobbling along the lane. He had a basket in one hand, and in the other was a stick on which he leant.

'Good afternoon to you,' he said to Joe. 'You are picking your berries quickly, young sir!'

'Yes!' said Joe. 'I want to fill two baskets, you see. My mother's going to make blackberry jam!'

'I wish I could pick as quickly as you!' said the little man. 'My back's so bent that I can't reach here, there and everywhere as you do! I get so tired!'

'Haven't you anyone to pick the berries for you?' asked Joe.

'No,' answered the little fellow, and began slowly to pick the blackberries.

'Look here!' said Joe. 'I believe, if I work hard enough, I'll have time to fill your basket as well as my two. Sit down and rest, and I'll try.'

'Thank you a thousand times!' said the little man, and sat down on the grass.

Joe picked here and there, and was delighted at the size of the lovely blackberries he found. Bigger than ever he'd seen before, he thought.

Just as the sun was slipping over the edge of the world, Joe gave back the little man's basket. It was full to the brim, and so were his mother's baskets.

'Here you are,' said Joe cheerfully. 'Nice and full, isn't it! And I hope your jam will be sweet and good.'

'Thank you,' said the little man, and felt in his pocket. 'Here's two shillings for you.' Joe went red.

'I don't want it, thank you,' he said politely. 'I did it because I wanted to help you, and not for any money.'

The little man smiled.

'You're the sort of boy any mother ought to be proud of!' he said. And then, to Joe's astonishment, he caught up his blackberries and went off down the lane, chuckling to himself just like a kettle on the boil!

Joe went home and showed his mother the two full baskets. She was delighted. She emptied the blackberries on to the scales to weigh them.

Suddenly she caught sight of something shining among the berries. It was two shillings. She picked them out and looked at them.

'Joe, Joe!' she called. 'There's some money in the basket among the blackberries! However did it get there?'

Joe started in surprise. Then he remembered the little man. He must have slipped them in among Joe's blackberries somehow, after all!

Joe told his mother about how he had filled three baskets with blackberries, and his mother listened.

'You're a good boy, Joe!' she said. 'Take the money. It's yours. Go and buy that yellow tractor you wanted.'

Joe took the coins and smiled. He wasn't going to spend it on a tractor; no, not he! He'd buy some big yellow pears for his mother, she was so fond of them! Off he went to the greengrocer's. He bought a big bag of pears for his mother, and turned to go home. He stopped outside a toyshop. There was that lovely tractor in the window.

Then he caught sight of a little box of crayons. Just what his brother wanted!

'I'll get them instead,' said Joe to himself. 'Jim doesn't deserve them, but, still, he hasn't got two shillings like me!'

Joe bought them and took them home with him.

'Here you are, Mum!' he said, giving her the bag with the pears inside. 'And here you are, Jim.'

His mother opened the bag, and cried out in delight. She shook the pears out on to the table, and marvel of marvels, a yellow tractor rolled out too!

What an extraordinary thing! Joe stared in surprise. But more amazing still, in Jim's parcel lay a beautiful little paintbox, side by side with the crayons!

'It's magic,' said his mother, smiling. 'You did a good turn to a gnome, Joe, and he's paid you a good turn back! Well, you deserve it!'

She kissed him and gave him the tractor and the paintbox. Jim looked on, feeling envious and really rather surprised.

'I wish I'd gone blackberrying too!' he said. 'Anyway, I shall go tomorrow!'

So the next day, off he went with a basket to the same place where Joe had gone the day before.

Sure enough, he had hardly begun picking when up came the little man, leaning on a stick.

'Good afternoon to you,' he said to Jim. 'You are picking some very fine blackberries, young sir!'

'Yes, I am,' said Jim. 'Do you want me to pick some for you?'

'Perhaps I do,' said the little fellow cheerfully.

'Will you give me two pounds if I do?' asked Jim greedily.

'Perhaps I may,' answered the little man, chuckling into his beard. 'Perhaps I may.'

So Jim picked berries until he had filled the little man's basket. *At least it wasn't really filled, but it would do*, Jim thought.

'Here you are!' he said at last. 'Where is my money?'

'Here it is, here it is!' grinned the little man, pressing two coins into Jim's hand. Then, with a thank you, he caught up his basket, and went off chuckling just like a kettle on the boil.

Jim didn't wait to fill his mother's basket. He was so anxious to spend the money. He ran home and showed his mother and Joe what he had got.

'Now I'm going to spend it!' he said, and ran off.

He spent it very carefully. He bought a bag of bull's-eye peppermints, because he loved them. Then he bought some very large apples for himself. He went to the toyshop and bought a box of soldiers, and with the last of his money he bought a colouring book.

Then, carrying all his treasures, he went home. He

took them up to his bedroom, for he was a selfish boy and didn't like sharing his things.

He opened the bag of peppermints – and oh! He could hardly believe his eyes. They had changed into stones! Yes, round, hard stones, not a bit of good for eating. His cry of astonishment brought his mother and Joe up to the bedroom, and they stared in surprise at the stones on the table.

Then Jim opened the apple bag – and out fell some turnips!

How his mother laughed!

'What have you bought turnips for?' she cried.

'They were apples when I bought them,' said Jim, half crying.

Then he opened his box of soldiers, but, oh, dear me! Inside was a big box of black medicine, and on it was written: FOR A GREEDY BOY.

Poor Jim hardly liked to open the colouring book parcel, but he did. Yes, it was a book all right – but not the one he had bought. It was called *Jim's Lesson*

Book and it was full of wise advice about selfishness and unselfishness, greediness and generosity. Jim went very red, and tears trickled down his cheeks.

'Never mind, Jimmy,' Joe said kindly, 'we'll read the book together.'

'I'm going to read the book from end to end!' sobbed Jim. 'I'm a horrid, selfish boy, and it's no wonder that little magic man laughed at me. I'll never be mean again – never, never, never!'

And so well did he keep his word that now there really isn't much to choose between Jim and Joe, outside and inside. They are twins that any mother would be proud of, thanks to that funny little man whose chuckling laugh was just like a kettle on the boil!

Foolish Caryll

Foolish Caryll

ONCE UPON a time, the king of the gnomes sent the fairy queen a wonderful singing bird for her birthday. It was in a beautiful cage of gold, and had one little door.

'Oh, *what* a lovely present!' said the queen. 'I shall call him Merrodel. Sing, Merrodel, sing!'

The little blue bird opened his orange beak and sang.

'Beautiful!' sighed the queen, when the song was finished. 'What a precious bird! I must have someone careful to look after him.'

'Please, Your Majesty, *do* let me!' begged a little elf. 'I'd love to!'

The queen looked at him. He was a dear little elf, but rather foolish sometimes.

'I don't know if I can really trust you to be careful enough, Caryll,' said the queen, 'but I'll try you.'

So Caryll was put in charge of the singing bird, and every day he gave Merrodel grain to eat and clean water to drink. He loved the little blue bird and used to talk to him.

One day Merrodel begged that Caryll would let him out to fly round the garden.

'I'll come back, truly I will!' he promised.

'No, no, I can't let you,' said Caryll, shaking his head.

'Well, Caryll, *darling*, just let me put my head out of the door and *look* outside!' begged Merrodel.

Caryll didn't think there would be very much harm in that. So he opened the little door and said Merrodel could take just a little peep!

Merrodel put his blue head outside and peeped. Then he put more of his body outside, and suddenly he spread his deep blue wings and flew right out of the cage, away into the garden, laughing and laughing!

Caryll was dreadfully frightened. He knew he ought not to have opened that door. It ought to be kept shut and bolted. He could not think of anything else to do but shut and bolt it now, and then he put his head on his arms and wept and wept.

The queen came running to see whatever the matter could be.

'Oh, oh!' wept Caryll. 'Merrodel's gone! Merrodel's gone! He wanted to live in the garden, and now he'll never come back again!'

'Why, I'm glad to let Merrodel live in the garden if he wants to!' said the queen. 'He'll sing better there than in his cage. But, Caryll! How *ever* did he get out? The door's shut and bolted.'

'Yes! I shut it when he was gone. I was so frightened,' said Caryll, drying his eyes.

The queen laughed and laughed. 'Oh, Caryll!' she said. 'Can't you see that it's no use shutting and bolting the door when Merrodel's flown away!'

The Treasure Hunt

The Treasure Hunt

ONCE UPON a time a very peculiar thing happened to Jo and Ben. They were sheltering from the rain under a thick ivy clump in Bluebell Wood, sitting quite quiet, when they heard two small voices whispering together nearby.

'I've put the treasure in the old poplar tree,' said the first voice.

'How shall I know which one?' asked the second voice.

'Go down Green Lane till you come to the two beech trees,' said the first voice. 'Go between them and walk in a straight line to a chestnut. Turn to the left by that tree and when you come to an elm, go round it to a plane tree. Turn to the right, and, in a line with a silver birch, you will see the old poplar tree where the treasure is.'

The voices stopped. The two boys under the ivy clump looked at one another in excitement. Treasure! They knew where it was! They would find it and take it home!

'The rain has stopped!' said Jo. 'Come on – it will be easy to find. I remember all that was said. Let's go to Green Lane and look for the two beech trees!'

Off they went to the lane – but alas, it was wintertime, and the trees had no leaves! The boys did not know the trees without their leaves. What were they to do?

'We'll go and tell our teacher and maybe she will help!' said Ben. So they ran to school. The teacher listened. 'Well,' she said, 'we will tell everyone your story – and see who is clever enough to find the treasure!'

So she told the whole class – and they set out to

look for the treasure, each with the directions carefully written out on paper.

Mary ran by herself. She knew the two beech trees well – their twigs were so pointed and sharp! She could not mistake them! She came to them and walked between them in a straight line. She looked about for a chestnut tree. She saw a great many trees standing together – which was the chestnut? Mary knew! A chestnut has such sticky fat buds, of course! She ran to the big chestnut and looked at her paper. She must turn to the left by it till she came to an elm tree.

She turned to the left and walked on, looking for an elm. She knew that the elm usually has twigs growing round the bottom of the trunk in a bushy sort of way. She knew too, that the elm twigs would be full of little brown buds, and some would be round and bead-like, holding the elm tree flowers. She must look for those!

Presently she came to a big elm and saw the small buds on the twigs. She went round it. Now she must look for a plane tree. How could she tell a plane tree? Well, it might have old dry balls on it, the dead fruit – and it would certainly have a trunk that looked as if someone had been pulling bits of bark off it, leaving bare places! Yes – Mary was right – there was the plane tree with its old balls dangling and its trunk looking patchy. She turned to the right, and walked to a graceful tree with a pretty silver-grey trunk – the silver birch. And then, sure enough, standing in a line with the birch was a tall tree which held its branches upright instead of outspread – the poplar! Mary ran to it – and in a hole at the bottom she found the treasure!

What was it? It was a crock full of gold. What a find! How Mary rushed back to school to show it to the others! They had all given up the hunt – because they didn't know the trees in their winter dress!

How many of the trees could *you* have found, do you think? Bring some twigs to school and see if you know their names!

The Little Old Toymaker

The Little Old Toymaker

THERE WAS once an old man who lived with his wife in a tiny cottage. He was called Stubby the toymaker, and he could make the loveliest toys. He liked making tiny toys the best – small chairs and tables for doll's houses, little beds for tiny dolls to sleep in, and things like that. He was very clever at mending broken dolls too. Whenever a doll's face was broken, or an arm or leg, it was brought to Stubby and he mended it lovingly.

Then came a sad time for the old toymaker. Nobody seemed to want his toys any more. All the children had unbreakable dolls which never needed mending.

People said his shop was old-fashioned, and they went to the big new stores in the nearest town. Stubby went on making his little chairs and tables, but nobody bought them.

'Stubby, dear, I don't know what we shall do,' said his wife. 'We have no money now, you know. You have not sold anything for two weeks. I cannot buy flour to make bread if I have no money.'

'Dear me, this will never do!' said Stubby, taking off his big round glasses and polishing them furiously. He always did that when he wanted to think hard, and right now he was thinking very hard indeed.

'Have you thought of an idea, Stubby?' asked his wife at last. Stubby nodded.

'Yes,' he said. 'But it isn't a very good one. You know, my dear, our shop window is very old and the glass is not good. Perhaps people cannot see my nice little toys very well through it. Suppose we set out some little chairs and tables and beds on the broad top of the old wall outside. Then everyone would see them!'

'That's a very good idea,' said his wife. 'I am quite sure that if people saw them, they would buy them. You really do make them so beautifully, Stubby dear.'

So out went the old toymaker and placed six little red chairs and a table to match on the top of the low stone wall outside. Then he put two small beds there as well, and his wife arranged the tiny sheets, blankets and pillows on each. They did look so sweet! The sun shone down on them and old Stubby felt quite certain that anyone passing by would come in and buy them at once!

But nobody did. Nobody even seemed to notice the tiny furniture. It was most disappointing.

'I'll go and fetch them in after we've had supper,' said Stubby. So the two sat down and had a poor supper of one cooked turnip out of the garden and a crust of stale bread. It was nearly dark when they had finished. Stubby got up and went out into the little garden to fetch in his dolls' furniture.

He walked to the wall and looked down at it in the

twilight. To his great astonishment there was no furniture there! It had gone! He felt all along the wall in dismay, and then hurried back to his wife.

'My dear!' he called. 'All my chairs and the table and beds are gone!'

'Has someone stolen them?' said his wife, almost in tears. 'Oh, what a shameful thing to steal from a poor old couple like ourselves!'

'Never mind,' said Stubby. 'It shows someone noticed them, anyhow. I'll put some more out tomorrow and I'll keep my eye on them!'

So the next day he put out a set of green chairs and a table to match, and one tiny bed. He sat at his window and watched to see that no one took them. But nobody seemed to notice them at all.

And then a strange thing happened. Stubby could hardly believe his eyes! He saw the chairs and table and bed walking off by themselves! Yes, really – they just slid down the wall and made off out of the gate!

Stubby ran after them. 'Hi! Hi!' he called. 'What

do you think you're doing?'

He made a grab at a chair – and to his enormous surprise, he got hold of a little wriggling figure that he couldn't see!

'Let me go, let me go!' screamed the little creature he couldn't see.

'Show yourself then,' commanded Stubby, shaking with excitement. At once the little struggling creature showed himself and became visible. It was a very small pixie!

'Bless us all!' said Stubby, his eyes nearly dropping out with amazement. 'It's the very first time I've ever seen a fairy! Pray what are you doing, stealing my chairs?'

'Oh, are they yours?' said the pixie in surprise. 'Hi, brothers. Stop carrying off this furniture. It belongs to someone!'

At once all the chairs and tables were set down, and many small pixies became visible before Stubby's astonished eyes.

'We are really very sorry,' said the first pixie. 'You see, we found the chairs, tables and beds on the wall there, and we didn't know they belonged to anyone at all. We thought they were very beautiful, so we took them into the woods to show the queen.'

'Dear, dear me!' said Stubby, flattered and pleased. 'Did you really think they were beautiful? And what did the queen think?'

'Oh, she liked them so much she said she would like ever so many more,' said the pixies. 'She has a new country house, you know, and she has been looking everywhere for furniture nice enough for it.'

'Well!' said Stubby, most excited. 'This is really lovely. You might tell the queen that I have a great deal more furniture if she would like to see it. I didn't put out my best pieces in case it rained.'

'Oh, of course we'll tell her,' said the pixies. 'Goodbye for the present, old man. Take your chairs, and table and bed – we'll go and tell the queen all you have said.'

Off they went, and Stubby took his toy furniture into the cottage with him and told his surprised wife all that had happened.

That night there came a knocking at his door – and when Stubby opened it, who do you suppose was there? Yes! – the queen, all dressed in shining moonlight with a silver star in her hair! She sat on the table and asked Stubby to show her all the furniture he had.

With shaking hands the old man set it out, and the queen exclaimed in delight. 'Oh, what beautiful things you make!' she cried. 'Just the right size for the little folk too. I suppose, old man, you are too busy to make things for us? The humans must be so pleased with your work that you will have no time for fairy folk.'

Then Stubby told the queen how hard he found it to sell anything, and his wife told her how little they had in the larder.

'We would be so glad if you could buy some of our goods,' she said.

'I can do better than that!' cried the beautiful queen

in delight. 'Stubby, come and live in Fairyland, will you? Please do! You can make all the furniture for my new country house. And there are no end of little jobs that your clever fingers could do really beautifully. I believe you could even patch up the wings of pixies when they get torn!'

'Oh, yes, I could!' said Stubby, his eyes shining brightly behind his big spectacles. 'I'll come whenever you wish, Your Majesty!'

So Stubby and his wife left their little cottage one fine morning and went to Fairyland. There the queen gave them a little white house on a hill. Stubby makes beautiful furniture all day long, and he often patches up the torn wings of the pixies.

And once a month he dresses himself up very grandly indeed, and so does his wife. For then the queen herself comes to tea, and each time there is a new little chair for her to sit on. She is so pleased.

Sally
Suck-A-Thumb

Sally Suck-A-Thumb

ONCE THERE was a little girl called Sally Suck-A-Thumb! Guess why! Well, you guessed right if you said it was because she would keep sucking her thumb.

You know, some children suck their thumbs and some don't when they are little. Sometimes they suck their thumbs because they are lonely or unhappy, and sometimes just because it's a habit they can't get out of.

Well, Sally wasn't lonely and she wasn't unhappy either. She was just an ordinary jolly little girl with plenty of toys and friends – and a thumb she sucked half the night and half the day!

'Don't suck your thumb, Sally,' said Mummy. 'Babies suck their thumbs! You are a big girl.'

Sally took her thumb out of her mouth. In half a minute it was in again! You see, she just couldn't remember.

'You know, Sally,' said Granny, 'you are growing your nice new teeth in front – your second, grown-up teeth. If you keep putting your thumb in your mouth to suck, it will push your growing teeth outwards, and you will have rabbit-teeth, sticking out over your lip. You wouldn't like that, would you?'

'No,' said Sally, and she took her thumb out of her mouth at once. But in half a minute it was in again! Poor Sally Suck-A-Thumb! How she wished she could remember not to suck that little pink thumb.

Sally was a kind little girl. She was always doing nice things for people, and one day she did something kind for an old lady she met down Cuckoo Lane.

Sally didn't know the old lady was half a fairy, because, except for her bright green eyes, she looked just like any other old lady.

She was carrying a big basket of all kinds of things, and suddenly a cow behind the hedge mooed very loudly indeed. The old lady had a fright, tipped up her basket, and out fell all the things she had bought!

'Oh, dear, oh, dear!' she said. 'Look at that! I must pick them up again, and I do find it so hard to bend down now I'm old and stiff.'

Sally saw and heard all this and she ran up at once. 'I'll pick everything up for you,' she said. 'I'd love to.'

She picked up the butter. She picked up the tea and the sugar. She found where all the potatoes had rolled to. She discovered a tin of polish lying under a clump of nettles, and had to let her hand get stung by them when she picked it up.

'Oh, you're stung!' cried the old lady. 'Let me see.'

Sally held up her hand. The old lady looked at it. 'Was it the thumb that got stung?' she asked. 'It looks rather red and sore.'

'No; that's only because I'm always sucking it,' said

Sally. 'I love sucking my thumb, you know.'

'How funny!' said the old lady. 'I would much rather suck toffee, or something like that.'

'Oh, well, so would I,' said Sally. 'Though my very favourite sweet is peppermint rock. You know – the kind you get at the seaside. I simply *love* that.'

'Do you really?' said the old lady. 'Well, in return for *your* kindness, little girl, I'll do *you* one – you shall have peppermint rock to suck all day and night long, if you want to!'

'Oh, thank you,' said Sally, thinking that the old lady meant to give her some. But she didn't. She just picked up her basket, nodded her head at the little girl, and trotted off down the lane.

Sally stared after her. What did she mean about having peppermint rock to suck all day and night long? The little girl popped her thumb into her mouth as usual and thought hard.

And, dear me, what a very, very extraordinary thing – her thumb tasted of peppermint rock!

Sally could hardly believe it. She took her thumb out of her mouth and looked at it – and, do you know, it had gone that funny reddish-pink colour that all peppermint rock is, on the outside.

'I do believe my thumb is made of peppermint rock!' said Sally in the greatest surprise. She popped it into her mouth again. Yes – the more she sucked her thumb the more she tasted peppermint rock. How very, very nice!

She ran home to tell her mother. Her mother couldn't believe that such a funny thing had happened, but when she tasted Sally's thumb herself she found that the little girl was right – it was made of peppermint rock!

But then Sally's mother looked very serious and solemn. 'If it's peppermint rock,' she said, 'you will suck it all away, Sally! You know, sweets don't last for ever! What will you do without a thumb?'

Sally stared at her mother in dismay! Good gracious! She hadn't thought of that! She popped her thumb into her mouth as she always did when she thought hard. But at once she took it out again. This would never do! She must *not* suck away her nice, useful little thumb!

'Oh, Mummy! The old lady thought she was doing me a good turn, but she wasn't,' said Sally, half crying. 'She forgot I might suck my thumb away! Now I shall never dare to put it into my mouth. Already I think I've sucked it thinner since it was peppermint rock.'

'Well, darling, for goodness' sake do remember not to suck it any more,' said Mummy anxiously. 'And as soon as you see the old lady again, tell her she did you a *bad* turn, not a good turn, and ask her to take away your peppermint thumb and let you have your own proper one.'

But, you know, Sally didn't see the old lady for weeks and weeks, though she looked for her every day. And all that while Sally didn't suck her thumb, because as soon as she popped it into her mouth the taste of peppermint reminded her that she might suck her thumb right away – and at once she took it out again.

So, by the time she *did* see the old lady once more, Sally no longer sucked her thumb! She had quite got out of the habit, and people didn't call her Sally Suck-A-Thumb any more. Sally was very glad.

And then, one Friday, she met the old lady in the lane. She knew her at once because of her very green eyes. Sally ran up to her.

'Good morning!' she said. 'Do you remember me? You said you would do me a good turn and you gave me a peppermint thumb to suck – but it was really a very bad turn because I might have sucked my thumb all away!'

'My dear little girl!' said the old lady, her green eyes shining kindly. 'You are wrong. I *did* do you a good turn by giving you a peppermint thumb – because, you see, I knew you would be sensible enough *not* to suck it– and so you would quite get out of the habit by the time I next saw you! I am sure I am right.'

'Well – you are!' said Sally in surprise. 'I *don't* suck my thumb any more – I don't even want to – so you *have* cured me of the habit. Please let me have my own proper thumb again, for I know I shall never, never suck it any more.'

'Very well,' said the old lady. 'Have your own proper little thumb – but, Sally, if ever you *do* begin to suck it again, you will taste peppermint, and that will warn you to take it out at once!'

Sally looked down at her thumb – it was pale pink again, soft and warm – not a peppermint-rock thumb any longer. How glad she was! She looked up to thank the old lady, but she was gone. Sally ran home to her mother.

'The old lady did me a *good* turn after all!' she cried, and she told her mother what had happened. 'I'm cured, Mummy, and I'm so glad.'

She *was* cured – but once, when she put her thumb in to suck a thorn out, what do you suppose she tasted? Yes – peppermint! Wasn't it strange?

A Wonderful Thing

A Wonderful Thing

DOWN IN the pond lived a big grub. Everyone was afraid of it. It lurked in the mud, staying very still, and then, when a tadpole or beetle swam too near, out would flash a pair of pincers and that would be the end of the tadpole or beetle!

One tadpole was not at all afraid of it.

'I shan't come near you!' said the tadpole. 'I shall keep away. One day I shall be a frog, grub, and I shall dive down into this pond and *eat* you!'

The tadpole grew his legs and became a frog. He left the pond one rainy afternoon and went to a damp ditch to make himself a new home.

But when the winter came he hurried back to the pond to sleep down in the mud. And there he saw the grub again!

'What! Are you still here?' cried the tiny frog. 'Well, don't you dare to try and eat me now. Next year I shall be very much bigger, and when I hop I shall startle everyone!'

In the spring the frog awoke and swam off to find himself a wife. She laid eggs for him, and put them in jelly so that the grub could not eat them.

The frog was bigger now. He spoke to the grub.

'This summer I shall be big enough to eat you, grub!' he said. 'I shall leave this pond soon and find my old home in the ditch, but one day in the late summer I shall come back and look for you, because I shall be ready to eat you!'

So one day in the late summer the frog went back to the pond to find the grub. He sat on a flat lily-leaf and peered down into the water. And he saw the grub there, crawling slowly up the stem of a water plant.

'Ah! He's coming up! I'll soon eat him!' said the frog to himself, and waited. He saw the grub crawl slowly up the stem right out of the water. There he stood, clinging to the stem. The frog got ready to fling out his tongue and catch him.

But wait, what was happening? Something very strange! The grub was splitting himself! His skin split all down his back. The frog watched in surprise.

Out from the split skin struggled a crumpled-looking creature. It had damp, creased wings. What could it be? The frog watched in wonder. He had never seen anything like this before.

The creature tried to spread its wings to dry them. It clung to the stem tightly. It had six legs and a very large head with gleaming eyes. Its body was long and slender and gleamed beautifully in the sunshine.

'Why, you're lovely!' said the frog suddenly. 'How could something so beautiful come from a grub? What are you?'

'A dragonfly!' said the creature. 'I have to spend

two years in the pond as a water creature, and then I become a beautiful winged insect. Did you say you wanted to catch and eat me, frog? Well, try!'

The dragonfly spread its wings and flashed into the air, making the frog jump and fall into the water.

'I'll have you for my dinner!' cried the dragonfly, and snapped its jaws at the frightened frog. But, of course, it didn't really mean it. Off it went into the sunshine, gleaming and shining.

'Well, who would have thought of *that*!' said the frog, and went hopping back to his ditch.

His Little Sister

His Little Sister

JACK WAS nine and Betty was six. At home they often played together, but when they went to the park Jack wanted to play with the older children.

'I don't want to take Betty,' he told his mother. 'She's too little. She's a nuisance. I can't be bothered to look after her.'

'Don't be unkind, Jack,' said Mother. 'Big siblings must always look after their little siblings, just as parents must always look after their children.'

'Well, I don't want to,' said Jack sulkily. 'I'm playing with Harry and Lennie and Tim today. I don't want to take Betty with me – and if I do I shan't look after her, so there!'

'I am not going to listen to you when you talk like that,' said Mother. 'Anyone would think you didn't love Betty, and yet I know you do. Now don't let me hear another word – take Betty and go.'

Jack went out sulkily, dragging poor Betty by the hand. Betty was sad. She did so like going with Jack, and it was horrid not to be wanted. 'I won't play with you and the boys, Jack, really I won't,' she said to him. 'I'll keep out of your way.'

'You'd better!' said Jack roughly. 'I'm not going to bother about you at all!'

As soon as he saw Harry, Lennie and Tim he let go Betty's hand and ran off with them. Betty went and sat down on a seat by herself. She felt very miserable. There were no other children to play with. So she sat still and quiet, watching Jack and his friends play.

Jack had a lovely game of cricket. He batted, bowled and fielded, and everyone shouted that he was jolly good. When he had made fifty runs he really felt like a hero.

'You'll be playing for England one day!' said the boys, and Jack felt grand. The morning flew and at last it was time to go home. He looked round for Betty. He had seen her on that seat over there.

But she wasn't there any more. Then where was she? She wouldn't have gone home alone because she had faithfully promised Mother never to do that. She must be somewhere in the park.

Jack hunted all over it. He called and yelled, but Betty didn't come. Suppose somebody had stolen her? People did steal children sometimes. Jack's heart went quite cold when he thought of somebody stealing his little sister.

Perhaps she had fallen into the duck-pond and nobody had heard her calling. He rushed to it and looked anxiously in the water. No Betty there, thank goodness.

Then *where* had she gone? He couldn't possibly go

home without her. Whatever would Mother say! And Daddy would be simply furious. Betty, Betty, Betty, where *are* you?

It was no use looking in the park any more. Betty must have left it. Oh, dear, there were all those roads to cross, if she had tried to go home. She would be sure to be knocked down if she went by herself. Suppose she was even now lying in some hospital with a broken leg or a hurt head?

Jack felt his eyes fill with tears. It would be all his fault, because he hadn't taken care of her. He went homewards, stopping at each of the crossings to ask the passersby the same question.

'Please – there hasn't been an accident to a little girl just here, has there?'

He got all the way home without hearing a word of Betty. He was so upset and miserable that he began to cry as soon as he saw his mother.

'Mother! Something's happened to Betty! She's lost – she's been stolen – or knocked down! Oh,

Mother, I was so cross with her, and I didn't take care of her and now she's gone. I've come home without her.'

'Poor Jack,' said Mother. 'How dreadful you must be feeling.'

'No, no – it's poor *Betty*!' cried Jack. 'What shall I do? Oh, Mother, I'm so sorry I was unkind. I wish, I wish, I wish I could see her this very minute – I'd always take care of her, always.'

Mother opened the door of the dining room and Jack went in, sobbing. There, sitting at the table, eating her dinner, was Betty, happy and cheerful!

Jack rushed at her and hugged her. 'Betty! Oh, Betty! I'm so glad to see you. I thought you were lost and gone for always.'

'Auntie came by and saw me by myself on the seat,' said Betty. 'When she saw you were busy with the other boys she took me to buy me an ice. Why are you crying, Jack?'

'I'll always take care of you, Betty,' said Jack,

so glad to see his little sister safe and sound that he could hardly stop hugging her. 'I'm your big brother, and you will always be safe with me.'

'That's what the *best* big brothers say,' said Mother. And she was right. They do!

In the King's Shoes

In the King's Shoes

ONCE UPON a time the magical brownie pedlar Twiddles was sitting down by the lane side mending a kettle. As he sat there who should come along but the king of Fairy Land himself! He was walking slowly, as if he were tired. He saw Twiddles sitting by the lane side and he sat down by him.

'Your Majesty, can I run to the nearest cottage and get a chair for you? said Twiddles, jumping up and bowing.

'No,' said the king. 'Let me sit in the grass for once if I wish to. My shoes hurt me. I shall take them off for a few minutes while I talk to you.'

The king slipped off his beautiful, highly polished shoes with their silver laces.

'My word!' said Twiddles the pedlar. 'I'd dearly love to be in your shoes for a little while, Your Majesty.'

'You would, would you?' said the king. 'Well, it's a silly, foolish wish of yours, but I'll grant it! Get into my shoes – and you'll find yourself king! I'll be a pedlar for a few happy hours!'

Hardly believing his ears, Twiddles got into the king's shoes. They fitted him perfectly. He stood up and gazed down at himself in astonishment. He was dressed like a king – and the king was dressed like a pedlar! Such was the magic in the king's shoes! Whoever wore them could be the king himself!

'Go down the lane and you'll meet my servants,' said the king. 'Good luck to you! I'm going to have a snooze in the shade here and listen to the birds singing.'

Twiddles went down the lane, holding his head high and looking as proud as could be. He was king! King! How grand it felt!

He saw some men hurrying towards him.

'Your Majesty, Your Majesty!' they cried. 'You will be late for the opening of that sale of work. Hurry, sire!'

Dear me, thought Twiddles, *so I am to open a sale of work, and everyone will bow to me and cheer me. How fine!*

He hurried to a waiting carriage and climbed into it. He drove off quickly to the next town. How the people there cheered him! He opened the sale of work, and read a speech that was put before him. He stood in the hot sun for about an hour, shaking hands with all kinds of magical brownies. He began to feel tired.

'I say, isn't it about time for dinner?' he asked a courtier nearby.

'Not nearly,' said the brownie, looking surprised. 'You have to review your troops of Scouts next, Your Majesty. Have you forgotten?'

Oh, well, thought Twiddles, *it will be fun to ask the Scouts all about their camp fires and the best way to boil kettles on them. I am sure I could teach them a thing or two about that!*

But, to his surprise, when he began to talk to the Scouts about this sort of thing his courtiers nudged his arm and frowned.

'Your Majesty is not supposed to know how kettles are boiled or camp fires made!' they whispered. 'Those are not the sort of things a king is interested in.'

Dear me! thought Twiddles. *How dull it must be to be a king all one's life! How hungry I am getting! Whenever are we going to have dinner? I guess it will be a fine one, with lots of marvellous things to eat and drink!*

But, to his great disgust, as soon as he had finished with the Scouts he was hustled into his carriage and driven off to see a new ship being launched – and a footman presented him with a little packet of sandwiches to eat!

'Is this all my dinner?' asked poor Twiddles. 'Just sardine sandwiches? Well, well, well! I'd be better off if I were a pedlar! I'd at least fry myself bacon and eggs, with an apple or two to follow!'

'Your Majesty, there is no time for you to have a proper lunch today,' said the courtier who was with him. 'You have to be at the dockyards in half an hour. And after that you have to visit a hospital. And then there is the flower show to go to.'

'Do you mean to say that all these things are on one day?' asked Twiddles in disgust. 'Don't I get any time off at all?'

'Your Majesty is acting very strangely today,' said the courtier, looking troubled. 'You promised to do all these things – and a king must keep his promise.'

Twiddles launched the new ship. He rushed off to the hospital, and walked round and round the wards, and spoke to everyone in the beds there. By the time he had finished his feet felt as if they could not walk another step, and his face was stiff with smiling so much. He badly wanted a cup of tea.

But no! He had to go to the flower show next, and miss out his tea altogether! He was still very hungry, as he had only had the sandwiches for dinner.

He yawned and yawned at the flower show, and his courtiers looked most disgusted with him. He didn't at all want to see the beautiful flowers they showed him. He didn't want to smell any of them. He just wanted to sit down on a chair and have a cup of tea all by himself.

When the flower show was over he was driven to the palace.

Twiddles was thrilled to see it shining in the evening sun. The people cheered him as he passed. Twiddles forgot about his dull and tiring day and waved his hat to the people. But that was not the thing to do at all. He had to bow stiffly from left to right and from right to left. He got out of the carriage and went up the long flight of steps.

'I want a jolly good meal now,' he said to the courtiers.

They looked surprised. 'Your Majesty, you will only just have time to change into your best uniform and get ready for the big military dinner you are giving tonight,' they said.

Oh, well, thought Twiddles, *I shall certainly have something to eat at the dinner – and I shall look very handsome in a uniform too.*

The uniform was tight and stiff. It cut him round the legs. It cut him across the shoulders. It was heavy. But still, he did look very handsome indeed. He went down to the dinner.

But before he could sit down he found that he had to shake hands with two hundred guests! Twiddles was not used to shaking hands with so many people and his hand soon ached terribly. At last he sat down to the table.

He had a famous general on one side, and a famous prince on the other. They both talked so much that Twiddles hardly had time to eat anything, because he had to keep saying, 'Yes, certainly,' and, 'No, of course not!' almost every moment.

The dinner took a long, long time. Twiddles got

very bored. He thought the general and the prince were both very silly. He wished they would stop talking for just one minute. But they didn't.

At last bedtime came. Twiddles felt as if he was being squeezed to death in his tight uniform. He could hardly breathe. He was so very, very glad to get out of it. His servants left him when he was ready for bed. He stood and looked at the beautiful bed ready for him – and he shook his head.

'No,' said Twiddles. 'I don't want to sleep in you – and wake up in the morning to rush about all day long doing things I don't want to do. It's a difficult thing to be a king. I'd rather be a pedlar. I'm free, but a king is not. A king has many masters and must do as he is told all day long – a pedlar has no master and is as free as the air! I'm going back to be a pedlar again!'

He slipped out of the palace in his sleeping suit. He made his way to the stables. He jumped on a horse, and rode bareback to the lane side where he had left the king.

There was a small light there – the remains of a camp fire. A man was sleeping peacefully beside it. It was the real king!

Twiddles woke him. 'Wake up!' he said. 'I've come back. I'm not a good king! I got hungry and bored. I'd rather be a pedlar.'

The king sat up and stared at him.

'Well, I got hungry and bored too, when I was a king,' he said. 'I like being a pedlar. It's lovely! Just do what you like, and nobody to say, "It's your duty to do this or that!" No, Twiddles, you go on being a king. I don't want to go back.'

Twiddles kicked off the king's shoes. He had put them on to come back in. In a trice he had changed once again to the untidy pedlar he had been that morning. Even his beautiful sleeping suit disappeared and he was dressed in his same old clothes. But the king was dressed in the fine sleeping suit – he was no longer a pedlar!

The king got up. 'Well, well,' he said, 'I suppose I

had better go back. After all, it's my job. I must do it as well as I can for the sake of my people, who love me. But oh, pedlar, you can't think how I have enjoyed today!'

'Yes, I can,' said Twiddles, patting the king kindly on the back. 'You've enjoyed today just as much as *I* shall enjoy tomorrow. Now, goodnight, Your Majesty, and pleasant dreams!'

Twiddles lay down by the fire. The king galloped back to the palace on the horse. And when the pedlar awoke next morning he wasn't at all sure that it was nothing but a dream!

'Poor old king!' he said. 'He has the hardest job in the world. Won't I cheer him when I next see him! But I wouldn't be in *his* shoes for anything!'

The Ship in the Bottle

The Ship in the Bottle

UNCLE TOM had something very strange on his mantelpiece. When John and Robert went to stay with him it was always the very first thing they looked at.

It was a fully-rigged ship inside a bottle! The boys looked and looked at it. They simply couldn't make out how the ship got into the bottle.

'It nearly fills the bottle,' said John, 'and yet the neck of the bottle is so narrow that nobody, nobody could get the ship through it – so how did the ship get there?'

Uncle Tom didn't know either. 'Must be magic!' he said. 'I don't know how it's done. Your aunt bought it at a sale one day and there it's been ever since, sailing away on my mantelpiece, inside the bottle! It's a lovely thing, isn't it? Your aunt is very fond of it.'

Aunt Julia came into the room. 'Are you two boys staring at that ship again! I believe you like it better than anything in the house. I like it too – it's strange, isn't it? Goodness knows how the ship got into the bottle but there it sails, year in and year out.'

'I guess it wishes it could sail just for once on real water,' said Robert. 'It's a proper little ship, Aunt Julia, and all the sails are exactly right, all fully-rigged and set correctly. It's a marvel, that ship!'

'Well, don't you mess about with it,' said Uncle Tom. 'I don't want the bottle broken – the ship would break then too.'

When Dick from over the road came to tea the boys showed the ship to him. Dick stared at it in surprise. 'A ship inside a bottle! I've never seen that before. I say – it's strange, isn't it? How did it get there? Nobody could get a ship as big as that through the neck of the bottle.' He picked it up, and the two boys shouted at him at once.

'Don't touch it! Put it back!'

But Dick was obstinate. He held it in his hand and examined it closely. 'All those sails full set,' he said, 'and the mast—'

'Put it back!' said John fiercely, and he snatched at it. Dick held on, and swung himself round to get away from John's hand. He caught his foot in the hearth rug and fell over.

Crash! The bottle fell to the floor and broke neatly in half. The little ship stayed in one half, for it was stuck tightly there – but the top of its main mast was broken off.

The three boys stared down in dismay. 'You fool!' said John angrily. 'Look what you've done!'

'If you hadn't grabbed at me it wouldn't have happened,' said Dick sulkily. 'It's all your fault.'

'It isn't! It's your fault for taking the bottle off the mantelpiece in the first place,' said John fiercely.

'My uncle will be furious. You can jolly well go and own up.'

'Well, I'm not going to,' said Dick, stalking out of the room. 'It *wasn't* my fault. Just like you to try to put the blame on someone else.'

He went out of the house and ran across the road to his own home. Robert and John looked at each other. 'Let's go and tell Uncle now,' said Robert. 'I bet Dick will get into a row.'

'Well – that would be telling tales, and Uncle doesn't like that,' said John. 'Look, let's put the two halves together and get some glue or something. Perhaps we can mend it so that nobody will notice.'

'No. That's as bad as telling tales!' said Robert. 'You know it is! Oh blow! It was such a lovely thing and now it's spoilt.'

'Well – can we possibly get another bottle and put the ship into it somehow ourselves?' said John. 'Let's try. Somebody once put it in, so perhaps we can.'

'We could try that,' said Robert. 'Let's try at once.

Uncle and Auntie are out. We might be able to do it before they get back. Then it won't be so bad having to own up.'

They went to the cupboard where jars and bottles were kept. They took out an empty bottle very much the same as the broken one. Then, carrying the ship very carefully in one of the broken pieces, they went to their bedroom. John looked at the ship closely.

'Isn't it beautifully made?' he said. 'I'm glad it wasn't badly broken – look, only the mast-tip has gone. Now, the first thing is to get it off this broken half. Look how someone has painted a bit of wood the colour of the sea for it to sail on, Robert.'

They chipped the ship and the wooden waves carefully off the broken glass. Then they got the bottle they had found. But it was absolutely impossible to get the ship through the neck – it was far too tall, with its lovely masts and beautiful sails.

'No good!' said John, putting it down. 'Quite, quite impossible. But how did anyone ever get it into a bottle? It simply must be magic.'

'Hello!' said Aunt Julia, suddenly opening the door. 'I wondered where you were. Oh – surely, surely you haven't taken that ship out of the bottle! However did it get broken?'

'Well, it fell on the floor,' said John, going red. 'And the bottle broke.'

'I told you not to take it off the mantelpiece,' said Aunt Julia, vexed. 'I'm surprised at you. You know how fond of that ship Uncle and I are.'

Robert longed to say it was Dick who had broken it, but John frowned at him. He did so hate telling tales. The boys at school hated a sneak but all the same it was very hard to take the blame for somebody else.

'It's no good trying to poke it into that bottle,' said Aunt Julia, still very cross. 'You'll only break the whole ship up. I really do feel annoyed with you. I only hope Uncle won't send you back home. You know what he thinks of disobedience!'

She went out of the room. The two boys felt

alarmed. It would be dreadful to be sent back home in disgrace. But John soon cheered up.

'Aunt Julia wouldn't send us home. I know she wouldn't. She's cross now, but she's very kind really. I wish we could do something to make up for this – even though it isn't our fault.'

'Let's tell Auntie it was Dick,' said Robert. 'Anyway, if Uncle says he's going to send us home, will you tell then?'

'Well, I might then,' said John. 'Look, I'll tell you what we'll do. I'll get the mower and mow the grass for Uncle before he comes home and you go and clean Aunt Julia's garden tools. That'll be just a little something to make up for the ship.'

So when Aunt Julia looked out of the window, there was John mowing the grass, and Robert busily cleaning her tools. She couldn't help smiling.

'Trying to show they're sorry, I suppose!' she said. 'Well, that's something! Naughty little boys!'

The ship was put into a cupboard because Auntie

said it would get so dusty now that it was no longer in a bottle. The boys were sad. 'Now nobody will see it again,' said John, 'except us if we go and peep at it. Blow it!'

Uncle had been cross, but not quite so cross as he might have been if his lawn hadn't been so beautifully cut! Nothing more was said about the ship. Auntie threw away the broken halves of the bottle, and was her own kind self again.

Two days later Dick came creeping in at the garden door to find John and Robert. He knew that their uncle and aunt were out. He looked rather shamefaced, and kept his head down when he spoke to them.

'I say – I saw your aunt and uncle go out. Are they very cross with me? Are they going to tell my dad? What did they say when you told them I'd broken the bottle?'

'We didn't tell them,' said John. 'We aren't sneaks. If you didn't own up, we weren't going to tell tales. We got into trouble for it, instead of you. You're mean. Aunt Julia said Uncle might send us home in disgrace.'

Dick raised his head in surprise at all this. 'What! Didn't you tell them I broke the bottle?' he said. 'Gosh, I've been worrying no end about it – that lovely ship – and being afraid your uncle would come over to my dad about it. I knew I'd get into trouble if he did. I didn't sleep at all the night before last.'

'Serves you right,' said Robert hard-heartedly. 'I wanted to tell. You're a coward not to own up! We don't want to play with you any more. Go on home.'

Dick went very red. He didn't like being spoken to like that. He looked at the mantelpiece. 'Where's the ship?' he said.

'In that cupboard, where nobody ever sees it,' said John. 'The broken bottle has been thrown away. Don't come over here again, Dick. We don't want you.'

Dick went, looking miserable. He sat and thought hard in a corner of his garden at home. He must own up! It was so decent of John and Robert not to sneak. What a pity he had broken that bottle with the ship inside.

He suddenly thought of something. Down at the jetty by the shore was an old sailor called Salty, who was very clever with his hands. He could mend any boat in the bay, he could make nets of all kinds, and his great thick fingers could even work with shells and seaweed, and make quaint treasures to sell to visitors. Would he know anything about ships in bottles? Perhaps he even had one to sell!

Dick took down his piggy-bank from the mantelpiece. It was a china pig with a slit in his back, and a little door in his tummy that could be unlocked. Dick didn't know how much a ship in a bottle was, but he was quite prepared to pay out every penny he had if he could get one. He thought that John and Robert had behaved in a surprisingly generous way, and he felt very small and mean. He would go on feeling like that till he somehow put things right!

He had two shillings in the pig. It seemed a large

sum to Dick. Surely that would buy a new ship in a bottle?

He went to find Salty. There he was, sitting on an upturned boat, busy at something. Dick went up to him.

'Salty, you haven't got a ship in a bottle to sell, have you?' he asked.

'No. It's a long time since I made one of those,' said Salty. 'Tricky things they are. Very tricky. Getting them into the bottle is a fiddly job!'

'Oh – do you know how to do that?' said Dick, suddenly excited. He told Salty all about the broken bottle and the beautiful little ship.

'Salty – if I bring you the ship, could you possibly get it into the bottle?' he asked eagerly. 'Could you?'

'Oh, ay. I couldn't make the ship nowadays but I know how to get one into a bottle,' said Salty. 'You bring it along and I'll do it for you.'

'Will you do it for two shillings?' asked Dick. 'That's all I've got.'

'Well, seeing that it was your fault the bottle got broken, you ought to pay something for it,' said Salty. 'You give me half the money. That'll be all right.'

'Oh, thank you!' said Dick joyfully, and ran off to find John and Robert and tell them the news.

They could hardly believe their ears. 'What! Salty knows how to get the ship into the bottle?' said John. 'How does he do it?'

'I didn't ask him. We could watch him,' said Dick. 'Where's the ship? Come on, let's take it and see if Salty really can do it!'

They took the little ship from the cupboard and raced down to Salty with it. He grinned at them, and took the ship in his great tanned hand.

'Ah – she's a tidy little ship,' he said. 'A little beauty. Look, I've got a bottle that will fit her well. Nice and clean it is, too.'

The boys stayed the whole morning with him, watching him. First he mended the top of the broken mast very cleverly indeed. Then he touched up the ship here and there with paint, so that she gleamed fresh and new.

Then he began to jiggle with the masts a little. 'What are you doing?' said John. 'Don't break them, for goodness' sake!'

Salty laughed – and at that moment one of the masts fell down flat on the ship's deck, taking its sails with it. The boys groaned.

'Now you've broken that mast,' said John.

'Nay – I haven't,' said Salty with a grin. Just then down went the second mast and the rest of the sails lay flat too!

'They're not broken – they're hinged at the bottom,' said Salty. 'Look close and you'll see. That's the secret of getting the ship into the bottle. Now watch!'

The ship's hull was set fast in the painted wood strip of the sea. Mast and sails lay flat. Salty picked up the ship and the bottle. He held the ship near the bottle neck and twinkled at the boys. 'See how easily she'll go in now the masts and sails are flat on the hull? Easy!'

'Oh, yes! She's small enough now to slip inside!' cried Dick. 'I never thought of that! But Salty – how will you get the masts and sails upright again, once the hull is in the bottle?'

'Ah now, you watch and see,' said Salty, putting down the bottle. The three boys bent their head over his deft fingers as he worked on the masts with tiny threads. He fastened a thread to each mast with a slip-knot.

'Now, watch again,' he said, and slid the hull of the ship into the bottle neck. It slid right through it into the main part of the bottle, where Salty had smeared some glue with a brush. It stuck there standing in the correct position. The threads from the fallen masts hung out of the neck of the bottle.

Salty pulled one carefully. The mast rose upright in the bottle and took the sails with it. He pulled the other thread and the second mast rose too. Now the little ship was in full sail!

Salty drew the threads out and threw them away. He sealed up the bottle and gave it to Dick.

'There you are!' he said. 'That's how all ships are put into bottles. No magic about it – just a little ingenuity and careful handling. Take care of it this time, and don't break the bottle!'

'Oh! That was well worth the money,' said Dick, delighted, and he took the bottle from Salty. 'Thank you. Come on, you others. I'm going to take it to your uncle and own up!'

Uncle Tom was amazed to see Dick holding the ship, safely in a bottle again. He listened gravely to what the boy said.

'I broke the bottle, and I wouldn't own up. And the others didn't tell tales on me so you didn't know. I'm sorry, Mr Gray. I've got the ship mended again. Salty did it!'

'Splendid!' said Uncle Tom and patted Dick on the shoulder. 'I'm glad you owned up. It's cowardly not to. John and Robert, I'm sorry I was cross with you, but I didn't know. And to think you mowed the grass and cleaned your aunt's tools too, so cheerfully!'

'Tom! They deserve a reward!' said Aunt Julia suddenly. 'Give them the ship! It would have been no use to us unmended and now it's so beautiful again, I think they should have it.'

So John and Robert have it for their own now, and it's on their mantelpiece at home. Did you know how a ship got into a bottle? I didn't – but I'm glad Salty told us all about it!

The Two Good
Fairies

The Two Good Fairies

DAVID AND Ruth lived in Primrose Cottage, and next door to them was Daffodil Cottage. An old man lived there, very fond of his garden, which was just a little piece like theirs.

One day the old man fell ill and had to go away to be nursed. David and Ruth peeped over the fence at his garden, which was full of daffodils and primroses.

'Old Mr Reed will be sorry to leave his lovely daffodils before they are over,' said Ruth.

'Mr Reed was a cross old man,' said David. 'He used to frown if we shouted or made a noise.'

'And he hated to let us get a ball if it went over the fence,' said Ruth.

'He was never well,' said their mother. 'That is why he was cross. I expect if he had been well and strong like you he would have been jolly and good-tempered.'

The cottage next door was shut up. There was no one to look after the garden, and as soon as the daffodils and primroses were over, the garden beds became full of weeds. The little lawn grew long and untidy, and thistles grew at the end of the garden.

'Isn't it a pity?' said Ruth, looking over the fence at the untidy garden. 'It used to be so nice in the summertime, full of flowers. Now it is like a field!'

'I wonder when old Mr Reed will come back,' said David.

'Mother says he is coming back in June,' said Ruth. 'Our garden will look lovely then, but his will be dreadful.'

'Let's go and buy our seeds tomorrow,' said David. 'We ought to be planting them now, you know, else our gardens will be late with their summer flowers.'

They emptied out their moneybox and counted their money. They had plenty to buy seeds.

'I wish we had enough to buy a nice wheelbarrow, a new watering can and a spade,' said David longingly. 'All our garden things are getting old. Shall we ask mother if she'll buy us some new ones?'

But mother said no. 'I can't afford it,' she said. 'I am saving up to buy a new mangle, because mine is falling to bits. I'll see about your garden tools after I've bought a new mangle.'

'Oh, dear,' said Ruth, 'that won't be for ages!'

The two children went off to the seedsman to buy their garden seeds. They bought candytuft, poppies, nasturtiums, virginia stock, love-in-a-mist and cornflowers – all the things that most children love to grow in their gardens. Then back they went to plant them.

They were very good little gardeners. They knew just how to get the beds ready, and how to shake the seed gently out of the packets so that not too much went into one place. They watered their seeds carefully and kept the weeds from the beds. Mother was quite proud of the way they kept their little gardens.

As they were planting their seeds Ruth had a good idea. She sat back on the grass and told it to David.

'I say, David, we've plenty of seeds this year, haven't we?' she said. 'Well, let's go and plant some next door in the little round bed just in front of the window where the old man sits every day. Even if his garden is in a dreadful state he will be able to see one nice flowery bed! It would be such a nice surprise for him!'

David thought it was a good idea. So when they had finished planting their seeds in their own little gardens the two children ran into the garden next door. Then they began to work very hard indeed.

The round bed was covered with weeds! So before any seeds were planted all the dandelions, buttercups and other weeds had to be dug up and taken away.

Then the bed was dug well over by David, and Ruth made the earth nice and fine.

Then they planted the seeds. In the middle they put cornflowers because they were nice and tall. Round them they put candytuft, with poppies here and there. In front they put love-in-a-mist with nasturtiums in between, and to edge the bed they planted seeds of the bright little virginia stock. They were so pleased when they had finished, for the bed looked very neat and tidy.

'There! That's finished,' said David. 'Now we've only got to come in and weed and water, and the bed will look lovely in the summertime! How surprised old Mr Reed will be!'

You should have seen how those seeds grew. It was wonderful. The children's gardens looked pretty enough, but the round bed next door was marvellous.

The cornflowers were the deepest of blues, and the candytuft was strong and sturdy. The virginia stock was full of buds.

'Old Mr Reed is coming back tomorrow,' said Ruth in excitement. 'Won't he be surprised!'

He did come back – and he *was* surprised! The children peeped over the fence and saw him looking out of his window in the very greatest astonishment. He saw them and waved to them.

'Hallo, Ruth and David,' he said. 'Just look at that round bed! Isn't it a picture? I was so sad when I came back thinking that I wouldn't have any flowers in my garden this summer – and the first thing I saw was this lovely bed full of colour. Do *you* know who planted the seeds?'

David and Ruth didn't like to say that they had done it.

'Perhaps it was the fairies,' said Mr Reed. 'I shouldn't be a bit surprised, would you? Well, I shall have to reward then for such a kind deed. I wonder whether one of you would come over tonight after the sun has gone down and water the bed for me? I don't expect the fairies will come now I'm back, do you?'

That evening the children took their old leaky watering can next door and went to water the round bed. Mr Reed watched them from the window. Ruth and David saw something by the bed – and what do you think it was?

There was a fine new wheelbarrow, and inside it were two strong spades and a perfectly splendid new red watering can. There was a note inside the barrow too, that said: 'A present for the kind fairies who gave me such a nice surprise.'

The children didn't know *what* to do. Did Mr Reed really think it was the fairies that had worked so hard? Oh, what lovely garden tools these were – just what they needed so badly. They stood and looked at them.

'How do you like your new tools?' shouted Mr Reed from his window.

'Oh, are they for *us*?' cried the children in delight. 'It says in the note that they are for the good fairies.'

'Well, didn't you act like good fairies?' said the old man, smiling. 'You gave me a wonderful surprise, and now I'm giving you one. You did a very kind deed to a cross, bad-tempered old man. But I'm better now, and so is my temper, especially since I've had such a lovely surprise. So I hope you will often come to tea with me and play with the new puppy I have bought. Now water my garden and then take your things home to show your mother.'

'Oh, thank you *so* much,' said the children, so excited that they could hardly hold the watering can properly. Whatever would mother say when she heard what had happened?

Mother was delighted.

'You deserve your surprise,' she said. 'You were kind to someone you didn't very much like, and now you have made a friend and had a lovely present.'

You should see David and Ruth gardening now with all their new tools. They are as happy as can be – and all because Ruth had a good idea and was kind to a cross old man.

The Wonderful
Conjurer

The Wonderful Conjurer

DAN AND Daisy had two white mice for Christmas. They were so pleased. The mice were dear little things, very tame indeed. One ran all the way up Daisy's sleeve, and she liked it.

And then a dreadful thing happened. One morning when the twins went to feed the mice in their small cage, they were not there! They had escaped.

'Look – there's a tiny hole there – they must have gone out through that,' said Dan. Daisy cried. She had liked the little mice so much.

'Cheer up,' said Mother. 'Think of something nice. That will help you to feel better.'

'Think of the party this afternoon,' said Dan, squeezing Daisy's hand. 'There's to be a wonderful conjurer.'

They went to the party at half past three. They had games first, then a lovely tea and then the conjurer came!

He was very, very clever. He made long ribbons come pouring out of his mouth. He cut a hole in a handkerchief, folded it up, opened it out – and dear me, the hole had gone!

Then he wanted two children to help him. Nobody would at first because they were shy. Then Dan and Daisy got up. They went to the conjurer, and he shook hands with them.

They helped him to do three more tricks, and he was pleased. 'Now comes my most amazing trick!' he said. 'I shall want your help here too. Now you, Dan, take hold of this box. That's right. And you, Daisy, put these two small white balls in the box, and then I am going to put on the lid. Then I shall tap three times on the box – and hey presto, when we open it, we shall find two white mice inside, instead of the balls!'

'They're the ones we lost!' cried Dan, and picked up one in his hand.

And so the twins took home the mice. Wasn't the conjurer a wonderful man?

Acknowledgements

All efforts have been made to seek necessary permissions.

The stories in this publication first appeared in the following publications:

'The Wish That Came True' first appeared in *Enid Blyton's Sunny Stories*, No. 477, 1950.

'The Magic Bicycle' first appeared as 'The Wonderful Scooter' in *Let's Read*, published by Birn Brothers in 1933.

'The Astonishing Curtains' first appeared in *Sunny Stories for Little Folks*, No. 149, 1932.

'The Grand Birthday Cake' first appeared in *Sunny Stories for Little Folks*, No. 220, 1935.

'The Flopperty Bird' first appeared in *The Teacher's Treasury*, Vol 1, published by the Home Library Book Company in 1926.

'The Wonderful Garden' first appeared in *The Teachers World*, No. 1828, 1938.

'The House in the Fog' first appeared in *Enid Blyton's Sunny Stories*, No. 495, 1950.

'The Magic Brush' first appeared as 'The Astonishing Brush' in *Sunny Stories for Little Folks*, No. 239, 1936.

'The Very Strange Pool' first appeared in *Enid Blyton's Sunny Stories*, No. 195, 1940.

'The Silly Little Conker' first appeared in *The Teachers World*, No. 1602, 1934.

'The Boy Whose Toys Came Alive!' first appeared in *Enid Blyton's Sunny Stories*, No. 195–196, 1940.

'A Pennyworth of Kindness' first appeared in *Enid Blyton's Sunny Stories*, No. 431, 1948.

'The Astonishing Ladder' first appeared in *Sunny Stories for Little Folks*, No. 161, 1933.

'The Impossible Wish' first appeared in *The Teachers World*, No. 1738, 1936.

'The House Made of Cards' first appeared in *Sunny Stories for Little Folks*, No. 164, 1933.

'The Salt, Salt Sea' first appeared in *The Teachers World*, No. 1625, 1934.

'The Goblin in the Train' first appeared in *Sunny Stories for Little Folks*, No. 128, 1931.

'The Box of Magic' first appeared in *Sunny Stories for Little Folks*, No. 235, 1936.

'The Unlucky Little Boy' first appeared in *The Teachers World*, No. 1831, 1938.

'The Little Silver Hat' first appeared in *Enid Blyton's Sunny Stories*, No. 234, 1941.

'The Toys' New Palace' first appeared as 'The Palace of Bricks' in *Enid Blyton's Sunny Stories*, No. 61, 1938.

'Blackberry Magic' first appeared in *The Teacher's Treasury*, Vol. 1, 1926.

'Foolish Caryll' first appeared in *The Teachers World*, No. 991, 1923.

'The Treasure Hunt' first appeared in *The Teachers World*, No. 1809, 1938.

'The Little Old Toymaker' first appeared in *Enid Blyton's Sunny Stories*, No. 12, 1937.

'Sally Suck-A-Thumb' first appeared in *Enid Blyton's Sunny Stories*, No. 190, 1940.

'A Wonderful Thing' first appeared in *Sunday Mail*, No. 1926, 1945.

'His Little Sister' first appeared in *Enid Blyton's Sunny Stories*, No. 410, 1947.

'In the King's Shoes' first appeared in *Enid Blyton's Sunny Stories*, No. 33, 1937.

'The Ship in the Bottle' first appeared in *Enid Blyton's Magazine*, No. 5, Vol. 1, 1953.

'The Two Good Fairies' first appeared in *Sunny Stories for Little Folks*, No. 191, 1934.

'The Wonderful Conjurer' first appeared in *Good Housekeeping*, Vol. 6, No. 6, 1946.

Also available:

Enid Blyton

STORIES OF
MAGIC
AND
MISCHIEF

30 stories

A spellbinding selection of magical and
mischievous tales by the world's
best-loved storyteller!

Enid Blyton

Look out for these enchanting
short-story collections…

Read them all!

Enid Blyton

is one of the most popular children's authors of all time. Her books have sold over 500 million copies and have been translated into other languages more often than any other children's author.

Enid Blyton adored writing for children. She wrote over 700 books and about 2,000 short stories. *The Famous Five* books, now 80 years old, are her most popular. She is also the author of other favourites including *The Secret Seven*, *The Magic Faraway Tree* and *Malory Towers*.

Born in London in 1897, Enid lived much of her life in Buckinghamshire and loved dogs, gardening and the countryside. She was very knowledgeable about trees, flowers, birds and animals.

Dorset – where some of the Famous Five's adventures are set – was a favourite place of hers too.

Enid Blyton's stories are read and loved by millions of children (and grown-ups) all over the world. Visit enidblyton.co.uk to discover more.

Illustration by
Laura Ellen Anderson.